Fifth Dan Taekwondo black belt, athlete, trainer, award-nominated television personality and popular author, Tiffiny Hall fuses a love of health and fitness with a passion for children's fiction. She has a Bachelor of Arts/Media and Communications and a Diploma of Modern Languages in French from the University of Melbourne. Tiffiny worked as a print journalist before writing her health books *Weightloss Warrior, Fatloss for Good: The Secret Weapon, Tiffiny's Lighten Up Cookbook* and *You Beauty!* Her debut novel, *White Ninja,* is the first book in the Roxy Ran trilogy, followed by *Red Samurai* and *Black Warrior.* She is also the author of *Maxi and the Magical Money Tree.* While writing her next novel, Tiffiny continues to work in television as a wellness expert and positive role model for women.

www.tiffinyhall.com.au

BOOKS BY TIFFINY HALL

ROXY RAN TRILOGY

White Ninja
Red Samurai
Black Warrior

Maxi and the Magical Money Tree

White Ninja

TIFFINY HALL

Angus&Robertson
An imprint of HarperCollins*Children'sBooks*

Angus&Robertson
An imprint of HarperCollins*Children'sBooks*, Australia

First published in Australia in 2012
by HarperCollins*Publishers* Australia Pty Limited
ABN 36 009 913 517
harpercollins.com.au

HarperCollins*Publishers*
Level 13, 201 Elizabeth Street, Sydney NSW 2000, Australia
Unit D1, 63 Apollo Drive, Rosedale, Auckland 0632, New Zealand
A 53, Sector 57, Noida, UP, India
1 London Bridge Street, London SE1 9GF, United Kingdom
2 Bloor Street East, 20th floor, Toronto, Ontario M4W 1A8, Canada
195 Broadway, New York NY 10007, USA

National Library of Australia Cataloguing-in-Publication data:

Hall, Tiffiny.
    White Ninja / Tiffiny Hall.
    ISBN: 978 0 7322 9453 3 (pbk.)
    For primary school age.
A823.4

Cover design by Blueboat
Author photograph by Peter Collie
Typeset in 10/17pt ITC Stone Serif by Kirby Jones
Printed and bound in Australia by McPherson's Printing Group
The papers used by HarperCollins in the manufacture of this book are a
natural, recyclable product made from wood grown in sustainable plantation
forests. The fibre source and manufacturing processes meet recognised
international environmental standards, and carry certification.

Dedicated to my little bro, Lleyton

AS A NINJA,
MY BODY IS A WEAPON,
MY MOVEMENTS ARE MAGICAL,
MY FOCUS IS LETHAL.
I AM THE INVISIBLE WARRIOR.

From the ancient ninja's Tiger Scrolls

ONE

'What's your egg say today, Roxy Ran?' Heroshi circles the playground bench where I sit. I know that his other friends will arrive soon and everything will happen again like yesterday.

I grip my lunchbox tight and squeeze my eyes shut, praying that the contents of my lunchbox are different today. But no such luck.

He grabs my hard-boiled egg and reads aloud the words written on it: 'Reach for the stars.' His voice, barbed wire, snarls into my hair. I brush my hair off my shoulders, then return my grip to my lunchbox. Even though my nails turn blue, I do not let go. I concentrate on breathing and will myself to disappear, to evaporate like steam on glass.

Shadow. Be a shadow, I tell myself, closing my eyes with the strain of making a wish. I feel myself break into a sweat. Shadows don't sweat. The disappointment turns my tongue to leather.

Heroshi cuts my lunchbox out of my hands with a turning knife-hand chop and it falls like a brick at my feet. His movement is swift and trained. Although he is only average boy height, his thick legs pose a powerful presence with each string of muscle wound to its maximum from years seated in martial arts stances; his legs look like they could snap lunchboxes, school bags, doors and necks. A year older than the rest of us in Year Seven, his martial arts skill is unmatched at school. Not only is he captain of the school martial arts team, he is also national champion. His school locker is shelved with trophies and medals that blind passers-by when he leaves the door open, which he does often. On Mondays and Wednesdays, when he has training, he wears his black belt under his oversized school jumper; you can just make out the embroidered tips hanging near his knees. Everyone calls him 'Hero' for short.

'Your mum should have written "fatherless",' he growls, hair like black onyx casting shadows across his stony eyes. 'Or maybe "father-*loser*", like you.'

The words slice me like a knife, as always. I've never met my father. Mum won't answer my questions, and there are no photos of him, no sense of him at all, around our apartment. The words are a log in my heart.

Hero's two friends arrive: Christian, known as Krew, and Bruce. Krew is tall and thick, driving his body like a monster truck, zit-skinned with ice-blond hair shagged over his eyes and hands like baseball gloves. Despite his gargantuan head, his eyes are the size of pins and they prick his pillowed face with a ghostly glare. Bruce, in contrast, is short and fast with thick brown curly hair barbed close to his brow. Crab-like, he is always poised with knees bent, scuttle-ready to pounce.

Something burns behind their eyes. Something stronger than hatred of the misfit; something stale … bruised … rotting. I thought this year would be different. But first term of Year Seven and I'm already bully roadkill. They all laugh, moving around me like sharks.

Hero is holding another of my hard-boiled eggs in his hand and showing its bald head to the sun. My mother's handwriting shines: *Fortitude*. I don't know what that means. She has signed the egg with a kiss; a kiss of social death.

'Nup, sorry, I was wrong,' Hero says, examining the egg more closely. 'It says your mum's boyfriend is an unemployed hobo!' He laughs, and his black hair is jagged shards of night. My pulse whips high. Red anger blisters my face.

Art's not unemployed, he's an artist, I want to say, but I cannot speak. Art has lived with us since I was five. He's not a martial artist like Mum, just an artist. My mother, a great shadow warrior, can slice the wings off a mosquito with a ninja star, but Art can paint rain on a road and make it look like another world. He's like a father to my sixteen-year-old sister, Elecktra, and me.

Mum's Japanese. Her dark almond eyes stand out against her fair complexion and blonde hair, like brown rocks against a glowing sunset. She's dyed her black hair blonde ever since I can remember. She says she gets to be a different person with blonde hair. When I asked if I could dye my hair blonde too, because I liked the idea of being a brand-new person, she said, 'You're Roxy with black hair like velvet, and it's beautiful.'

I wish I had blonde hair like Elecktra. My dark hair clogs the sink, whereas her golden hair slips through the plugholes like fine gold threads.

Sitting there, pinned to the bench, a sensation starts in my gut, a foaming fire that flushes into my veins, expands my muscles, scalds my insides and the soles of my feet. I move my hands from my lunchbox to the bench and clench it tight to anchor the fire in my gut. I can't let it reach my fists. Heat pulsates from the palms of my hands and burns into the wood. Two deep breaths and the feeling subsides to a wild grumbling.

Hero winds back his arm. I turn my head. A crash, the egg lies smashed across my knuckles, the word destroyed. The broken shells are on my hand: pieces of nude glass, shattered. The bell blares and Hero and the others split.

4

'Are you okay, Roxy?' My only friend, Cinnamon, comes rushing over, her red hair out of control today.

'I *am* such a loser,' I say.

She picks up my hand and wipes away the powdery yolk. 'Maybe you should ask your mum to stop giving you hard-boiled eggs,' she says. 'Maybe she could write on your sandwiches?'

'Won't make a difference. He'd throw anything at me. And Mum is so sweet with her "inspirational eggs".'

'Why's he hate you so much?' Cinnamon asks.

I stare at my lap, as if the answer might be woven into the yarn of my school uniform. I have no idea.

Where I've gripped the wooden slat of the bench, the wood has burned. I've been feeling this fire inside me ever since I turned thirteen, and it's become more frequent these past few weeks. I have to push it down because I fear that if I let it rise, I won't be able to control it. When I asked my sister, Elecktra, about the fire feeling, she said I'm probably going through an early midteen crisis.

Cinnamon's wild hair torches out from the edges of her face, the smouldering strands snapping with light as her freckles join across the bridge of her nose in the gauze-bright sun. I pack up my lunchbox and follow Cinnamon's flaming halo of hair to maths. I love Year Seven maths. There's no emotion in numbers, everything is reduced to circles and sticks and all of it fits in with each other. No anomalies. Unlike me and Cinnamon, total anomalies to every high school rule. We've known each other since Year Three, but didn't really become friends until high school, brought together by the shared shame of being the only Year Sevens not to make it through Gate One.

I don't know who started the Gate Divide, but it's existed since our school, Hindley Hall, opened. The school is in a huge mansion, a heritage building, that used to be a hospital. All the hospital rooms are now classrooms and music halls, and surrounding the mansion are clusters of modern single-storey classrooms with covered walkways between them. The walkways are paved in bricks with kids' names etched into them — like an honour board on the ground.

The main entrance to the school is through two large iron gates. Gate One, on the right, is for the cool, popular kids — those who can make skinny jeans look tough, anyone who knows how to tweet, anyone belonging to a clique or gang, athletic kids, or anyone with friends or allies in older years. Gate Two is for social misfits, weirdos and nerds. Geek chic skipped our school — we don't have anyone with a hidden talent for film-making or singing, just freaks who love medieval history or get overly passionate about the breed of their dog. Technically, I fit into the last Gate One category, because I have a sister in Year Ten. But Elecktra pretends we're not related.

I was pushed through Gate Two on my first day of Year Three because Mickela Grant (one of the popular girls) offered me a Redskin and I didn't know what it was. I tried to make it up to her by offering her half of my lentil rice wrap and some Hulk juice, but she called me a hippy and the damage was done. It didn't help that I was wearing a scrunchie in my hair.

Cinnamon is Gate Two because she's a little overweight, has porcelain skin covered in freckles and the most amazing red curly hair that looks like an afro wig. She makes no attempt to flatten her hair down or hide it, despite my sister's constant threats to ambush her with a hair straightener. And no one really likes sitting behind Cinnamon in class because they can't see the whiteboard.

Elecktra made Gate One on her first day at school because she wore boxer shorts under her school dress and that had never been done before. As anyone will tell you, she's also drop-dead gorgeous. She has luscious long blonde hair, dark brown eyes, long legs and the facial structure of a rosebud: small, glowing, compact and completely symmetrical. She walks out in front of traffic all the time because she's used to cars stopping for her. Elecktra never talks to me at school, and walks the last three blocks to the gates alone so we never arrive together. I'm not sure anyone even knows we're sisters, besides Cinnamon. It's fine by me. I'm determined to make Gate One someday on my own merit. I don't need the most beautiful girl in school, a 'fashionista', with her perfect complexion or pointless Facebook posts, to make me someone. I can do that on my own. Just gotta figure out how.

TWO

I wake with a gasp, remembering. My skull oozes sweat. Today is the worst day of term — casual clothes day. I sit up, panting with panic. I look around my room for something to tidy, something to distract myself. I start with the bed, folding the sheet with a knife-hand flick of the wrist, kicking the pillow to fluff it up and punching it to the head of the bed, then finally tucking the corners with a turning low block into a wrist lock so they look like hotel bed corners — just as Mum taught me. This is the way I make my bed every morning and it takes me exactly sixteen seconds. I begin to breathe more easily.

I search the room for something else to organise, but my shoes are in two neat rows next to the door, the paperclips on my desk are stacked in miniature towers and I re-ordered my books last night — by colour.

I switch on the desk lamp, leap to my desk and study it for a moment in the cone of light. I lift the right side and nudge it to the left. Straight. I open the right drawer and see the pencils loosely placed. I begin to order them in a line, grouping by colour and length. Then I duck to the floor and place my nose to the carpet. In the early powdery light, dust will sparkle; calling for a quick vac. Nothing has moved in or out of place since last night. I sigh. My room is always spotless, hospital clean and military tidy.

I'm not ready to face casual clothes day. Elecktra always insists on dressing me. Last term I rode my bike to school wearing one of Elecktra's outfits and I was so bullied I had to lie to Mum and say I ran into a parked car and fell off my bike. I had a cut on my cheek and bruises up my legs. I never told Elecktra that the reason my bike was smashed was because Hero kicked it in.

Year Seven has been my worst year yet. Hindley Hall covers Years One to Twelve, but it recently expanded and there was a big influx in my year. Everyone found a clique, except me and Cinnamon. The aerobics girls are too shiny and I don't do pigtails; the girls who spend all lunchtime reading magazines are too boring; the science and maths nerds think I'm too dumb; and I don't have the confidence to hang out with the theatre girls. When I speak to them, I never know if they're replying to me or in the middle of an improv scene.

I make my way down the spiralling black iron staircase that joins our bedrooms to the rest of our apartment. We live in a huge open-plan warehouse apartment that's painted bright yellow on the outside and has a picket fence enclosing a jungle of pot plants still in their plastic containers that Mum swears she'll plant one day, but she travels too often for work to get around to it. She's not a very good Stay-at-home Girlfriend. Art does most of the washing, ironing, cooking.

Inside, the warehouse has polished floorboards that always feel warm from the sun blazing in through three vast skylights. The kitchen, at one end of the apartment, is stainless steel with a monumental wooden table made out of old boat planking. The wood has been sanded, but you can still see the grain and flecks of colour showing what the boats used to be: turquoise cruisers, pink dinghies, sapphire yachts. I can sit for hours smoothing my hand across the grooves; it's as if I can feel the waves within them. Around the table sit eight iron stools, each seat painted with the face of an ancient Egyptian. Art believes furniture isn't just about the look, it's about lifestyle, and, according to him, the face stools say we're très chic. Elecktra and I think they're silly. I feel dumb sitting on some stranger's head, and I hate it that Elecktra always takes the stool with the woman wearing the crown, like she's some queen herself.

Sprawling out from the kitchen is the living room, with a green rug that looks like grass and shelves of books.

11

There's an antique cabinet where Mum keeps photo albums labelled with the years since Elecktra was born in 1996. Art's paintings coat the walls and reflect onto the floorboards, so it feels like you slide across his landscapes whenever you wear socks. If Art likes a painting, he'll leave it on the wall for a few weeks, even months. When he's over it, he paints the wall white and starts again.

Art is a very successful artist and has an exhibition every year. People even come from overseas to buy his paintings. After an exhibition, he always buys us presents. Last year he bought me a silver statue of a cat leaping off a pillar to a star. I love it because of my nickname, Cat, which comes from the birthmark in the shape of a cat on the right sole of my foot. Its tail curls around my heel, its face spreads across the ball of my foot, and its claws reach between my toes. It looks as though the cat is leaping across the arch of my foot. Elecktra always teases me about my 'cat tatt', as she calls it, saying it's why I'm such a 'softie'. Sometimes the fire feeling in my gut makes the cat turn red.

The warehouse narrows at the back to a corridor where the bathroom is located, under the spiral staircase that takes you upstairs to the bedrooms, all in a line down the corridor: Elecktra's, mine, then Art and Mum's. Each bedroom has a window that opens out over our next-door neighbour's house. Ms Winters lives in a brick two-storey home with a driveway and a clothesline in the backyard. The kind of house, Art says, that could turn out to be a prison if you let it clog up your creative tap.

'Breakfast is ready,' Mum calls from the kitchen.

I walk over to the boat table, which has been spread with warm supple pumpernickel toast, fresh organic eggs, fruit salad and two bowls of fluffy quinoa. It tastes like porridge but is a cousin of spinach, Mum says; and spinach is what she calls 'warrior food'. The cooking pans have already been washed and dried. Mum stands with a moss-green tea towel over her arm and a dagger in her hand. The blade traps the sunlight through the window above the sink and sends lasers of light into our eyes.

Art is already at the table. When I sit down, he ruffles my hair with a gentle hand. Mum begins to chop an apple at lightning speed. Most people would use a paring knife, but she prefers to cook with her ninja knives. She holds the dagger up to her mouth to inspect her teeth, then follows the blade with her eyes.

'I miss my knife-throwing days,' she sighs.

'So you've told us.' Art smiles and tucks into his quinoa.

Mum slices and dices the apple and throws the pieces into the blender on the other side of the kitchen. Every single piece makes it into the jug.

Art is already halfway through his fruit salad. 'Did you know concentration burns just as many calories as physical exercise?' he asks. I shake my head. 'That's why surgeons snack on jelly babies.' I look at him sideways.

Mum starts on the celery with a short sword, her fingers blurring like helicopter blades. With one swift movement she flicks the rings of celery off her chopping board and they fly, green bullets, through the air and land in the blending jug.

'Cat, can you please pass me a capsicum?' she asks.

I lean over a white ceramic bowl shaped like a piece of coral and select the brightest green capsicum. Only green fruit and vegetables are allowed in our morning juice — what Mum and Art call 'Hulk juice' because it makes you strong and it's green. Celery, capsicum, apple, broccoli and a dash of mint. I stand up to pass the capsicum to her, but she lifts her hand and stops me. I raise my elbow, pull the capsicum back to my ear, then spear it towards her. She watches it approach, then stops it with a palm hand strike. The pips explode and the flesh splits into stars. The pips fall to the chopping board, but the precision of her strike sends the green stars flying towards the blender.

My mother is ninja. She says she's only a retired ninja now, but weird deliveries still come to our house, we always get bailed up by Customs on family holidays and, like I said, she still spends a lot of time travelling overseas for 'business'. Mum's brought me and Elecktra up on a warrior diet and trained us in basic self-defence, but she's never taught us the secret ninja arts.

'Why haven't you trained me in ninja?' I ask, again.

Mum throws her sword into the chopping board and it pings upright.

'You don't want that life,' she says. 'Everything you love, you end up having to destroy. You can't always —'

I finish the sentence I've heard a million times before. 'Protect.'

'Hulk juice,' Art says, finishing the last of his fruit salad, 'is what has kept me going all these years.'

'Great for speed, strength and reflexes,' Mum says.

'Pass,' I say. I really don't like Hulk juice.

Art whips his head towards me. 'What's gotten into you? You used to love Hulk juice; now you sing your As. Paarse. Whaaaatevaaaar. Raaandom. She's watching too much TV! All those reality TV shows are affecting her speech,' he says, raking a hand through his hair.

I scrunch up my face. 'Whatever.'

He turns to my mother. 'Akita, I thought the "whatevers" were meant to start when she turned sixteen, like the older one.'

Mum smiles knowingly and takes Art's dirty bowl from him. He looks at her and she reaches across to touch the pink in his hair. They're obviously in love, I wish they'd just get married.

Art's been Mum's boyfriend since I was five. No other kid at school has a mum with an artist boyfriend. Art grew up in a cubbyhouse out in the bush, with parents who did yoga and worshipped the sun. They never married, so I doubt Art'll ever ask Mum, despite Elecktra's prompting.

One day we were all at the Gourmet Garage Café and when Mum went to the bathroom, Elecktra wrote on the specials blackboard *Akita! Will you marry me?* When Mum returned to the table, she squealed and hugged Art. Everyone in the café clapped until Art pointed to Elecktra, then looked at Mum with sad eyes and shook his head. Mum, in true unemotional ninja style, pretended it never happened, but it was still pretty embarrassing for everyone.

'Where is Elecktra?' Mum asks.

'Upstairs, grooming.' Art raises his blond brows to the skylights. 'Casual clothes day is the highlight of her year.'

Mum laughs.

I can only manage a corner of my toast spread with globs of tahini and smashed avocado. The mention of casual clothes day makes me feel sick. A little glass of Hulk juice appears next to my plate. Not helping.

Mum's hand is firm on my shoulder. 'Roxy Ran. One glass. That's all I ask.'

I pinch my nose with my thumb and forefinger, take a breath and slam the liquid down my throat.

'So,' Mum says, 'casual clothes day.' She takes the empty glass. 'Excited?'

'You should change that red T-shirt to yellow and honour your solar plexus,' Art offers. 'Yellow is the colour associated with your gut, which is where you hold anxiety. You'll have a much better day.'

Mum touches her stomach and sighs. 'That's right,' she says.

Art reaches a hand towards a yellow capsicum in the white bowl. 'We underestimate the power of colour.'

'Don't see it myself,' I say.

'Lecky, don't you think this is a bit much?' I say, flicking my eye patch up as my sister and I walk to school. I totally regret allowing Elecktra to 'style' my outfit. She selects a few kids each year from a Facebook lottery and for the past two years I've been unlucky. I flip the patch down again; at least with this I'll only see half the school population laughing at me.

Elecktra has her phone in one hand and is scrolling through comments on her Facebook wall. 'Post-apocalyptic future pirate chic is so right now. Trust me,' she says without looking up from her phone. 'I know fashion. This is just what casual clothes day needs — a bit of risk.'

The sky is bruised; it can't make up its mind to be blue or yellow. I feel those bruised colours inside me today; the colour of nausea, nervousness, ridicule. Art was right: my solar plexus feels grazed with anxiety.

'I admit the cape last year was a mistake,' Elecktra says.

I shudder. I've never been so mocked as I was wearing that stupid multicoloured sequined cape. 'I ended up on the worst-dressed list,' I say.

Elecktra huffs. 'Casual clothes day is serious business; it's the difference between thirty and 600 friends on Facebook, you understand?'

'Okay, okay, keep your tank top on,' I tell her.

Elecktra is wearing military-style, high-heeled boots, pink over-the-knee socks, an oversized T-shirt that says *I hate boys* in blue sequins and a cropped leather jacket. She carries a clutch purse instead of a school bag. On anyone else this outfit would look like a costume, but with her tall, lean frame she looks like a runway model. Her long blonde hair is messy, as if she's just woken up, although it took a whole morning of a combination of straightening wand, dry shampoo, curlers and blow dryer to achieve the relaxed look, and she's polished her cheeks with pink eye shadow to give them more of a glimmer than a blush. Casual clothes day is the highlight of Elecktra's social calendar. She's been posting potential outfits for weeks. The military boots and pink over-the-knee socks won with fifty Likes.

'I think my outfit is me,' she says grandly, as if addressing an audience.

'Who else would it be?' I ask with a flat look.

She ignores me and continues to address the fans in her imagination. 'In touch with who I am. Tough but feminine, military but boho, on trend but sophisticated.'

We'll be at school soon and I'm not ready to face it. I can't shake this festering feeling in my gut. Maybe it's the Hulk juice. I feel a heaviness descending down my forehead, an electric garage door closing.

Elecktra turns to me suddenly. 'Remember to tell the school gazette who you're wearing,' she says. 'Let's practise.'

'Do we have to?' I say, trying to swallow my nerves. 'I hate fashion.'

'Fashion is every day,' she snaps. 'Who are you wearing?'

'It's not the red carpet, Lecky.'

'Might as well be.' She stops walking and handbrakes my step with her arm.

My stomach flips. I have never felt like this before. It's no longer nausea, more a restlessness. I can hear my heart beating, feel the blood pumping around my body, my chest rising with every breath then collapsing as I exhale. I am hyper-aware of every pore rinsing oxygen and filtering dust. That Hulk juice must have been off. I try to walk away from Elecktra, but she holds me firmly until I relent.

'Dark-wash jeans, ballet flats, your red T-shirt, the cocktail ring you gave me to add ...' I forget the word I'm meant to use.

'Flair,' she says.

'And this eye patch.' I point to it. 'Oh, and hair and make-up by Elecktricity.'

'Elecktrafied,' she corrects me. 'It's my brand. Repeat.'

'Elecktra! We'll be late for school and I'm feeling wrong.' I try to tug my arm away, but she's strong. She drinks more Hulk juice than me.

I sigh. 'Elecktrafied.' She releases her grip.

'The patch adds mystery. If you want to be famous and popular, you have to create mystique,' she says.

'Where's your patch then?'

'I go MIA on Facebook once a month. I don't need a patch any more,' she says.

Suddenly, a hand grasps my shoulder. I freeze.

Elecktra's heeled boot flies past my face, a hand blocks it and I see my sister's clutch purse spin in the air as she steps into a deep tiger stance and blocks an incoming spear-hand strike.

'Mum! Seriously!' Elecktra yells, letting go her submission hold on our mother and bending to retrieve her fallen purse. 'You could have broken my phone!' She strokes it like a pet.

Mum stretches out her arm. She looks at me and shakes her head. 'Disappointing, Roxy.'

I roll my eyes. Having to walk to school with Elecktra every day is tough enough without Mum's surprise attacks to make sure we can defend ourselves. I can't believe I froze! All those Sunday afternoons of practice with Mum's blue noodle — a stick of foam she uses to make us block — and no real improvement. I'd love to tell Mum about the bullying at school. But being a ninja — I don't think she'd understand. She's probably never felt intimidated in her whole life.

Mum's wearing black running tights that show the definition in her strong, greyhound-like quads and a black puffer jacket with a hood. Her hair is tied up in a bun. She's not even sweating.

'We'll talk about this later,' she says to me. 'You'll be late for school — off you go.'

She sprints off, leaving us in a cloud of her perfume. 'Great roundhouse kick!' she yells over her shoulder to Elecktra.

'You know it,' Elecktra calls back. She bends down to gather the other contents of her clutch purse: a lip gloss, breath mints, worry dolls, a piece of quartz stone Art gave her and the doorknob to her bedroom. It's her very own security system; she carries it around so no one can get into her room.

'Want a bean?' she asks me. She's acting like nothing happened, just another episode in the reality TV series she's starring in, in her mind.

'Adzuki bean?' I ask.

Elecktra rolls her eyes. 'Adzuki beans are for losers. Jelly bean — here have the black one, I hate them.'

'Don't let Mum catch you eating sugar for breakfast. You know the rule.'

'Yeah, slows down my reflexes, blah, blah, blah. They were pretty good back there.'

She snaps her head back to elongate her neck and pops a handful of jelly beans into her mouth. I watch them slide down her throat. My mouth waters.

Elecktra shakes her head with a sugar buzz. 'So do you think Jarrod will like my hair?' she asks.

'What do you care if Jarrod likes your hair? He wants to leave Year Twelve to go full time at the car wash.'

I hate listening to her stories about boys. I know she only tells me as a rehearsal before telling her friends.

Elecktra stops walking for a second, throws another handful of jelly beans in her mouth and chews while thinking.

'It's like, the other day he said to visit him at work. So I went casual — flat boots, not heels.'

'What happened?' I ask.

'Well, nothing. But I told him what I wanted. I said, hey, I think we should act like grown-ups and if you want to be my boyfriend, just say so and I'll tell everyone. Make it official.'

'You did not say that.'

'No. But can you help me break up with Jarrod?' She grabs my arm and tugs on it. 'I'm *going* to say it to him.'

'Jarrod the car-washer?'

'I have another version with "loser" in it,' she offers.

'Are you even dating? And how many boys have I helped you break up with?'

'He walks in the gate with me every day. You know you don't walk through Gate One with just anyone.'

My heart folds in on itself as I think of the school gates. I dread going to school. It's exhausting. Not because of classes or PE, but because I'm nervous all day. I never feel completely comfortable. Sometimes I walk through the common area like I'm going somewhere really important and then just wait in the toilet for twenty minutes. If I look like I've got something important to do, I feel like people won't notice I don't have anyone to talk to. Other times I'll pretend to forget the combination to my locker. I'll look at the kids around me like, *Great — of all days!*, then I'll shrink my world to that tiny dial and lock out the laughter and the looks. If I'm dealing with my locker, I don't have to deal with them. The library is an option, but I can't go there every day. On really cold days the popular girls claim top spot in front of the heaters.

'Are you listening to me?' Elecktra shakes me gently.

I turn to her. 'Elecktra, do you ever feel like hiding?'

'Only if my mouthwash isn't doing its job.'

We reach the letterbox that flags we're only three blocks away from school. My hands begin to sweat and slide off the straps of my school bag. My stomach squirms. My tongue swells and grows bark. I stop and lean on the letterbox. The garage door slides down my forehead again, shuttering out light, air and sound.

'Not again!' Elecktra squeezes her clutch under her armpit, grabs my hands and puts them on the letterbox under my chin. 'Breathe,' she instructs.

I take a deep breath, but it strangles in my throat.

'Panic attacks just getting to school and you're only in Year Seven. How are you going to deal with senior school?' She rubs my back.

I squint my eyes and wish to be invisible. If I was invisible, I could walk through Gate One with Elecktra and it would be like I was popular and beautiful.

'I don't want to go. I look dumb.'

'You look like you.'

'That's the problem,' I squeak.

Elecktra pushes her water bottle under my nose and I take a sip.

'Soft drink!' I look at her, shocked. 'How'd you get that?'

'Chantell brings it to school for me. Her mum buys heaps of the stuff. Mum won't know. She's kidding herself with all that reflex food.'

The sugar bites the front of my brain and I feel it needle up my veins and into my neck.

'Good, huh?' Elecktra twirls on the spot. 'I'm going to get Chantell to bring me chocolate bars too! Imagine!'

The thought of seeing Hero and his mates, and me having nowhere to hide, makes my head too heavy to lift up off the letterbox. My hands grow piping hot under my forehead. My skin feels sunburned.

'C'mon, Rox, we'll be late again and I want to make an entrance.'

I turn my cheek onto the back of my hand. 'Will you walk in with me?' I ask, then close my eyes because I can't handle seeing her response.

'Stop asking me that. You know the answer. I'm going!' She pulls up her socks and walks off.

I slowly lift my head and look at my hands. They're burning with the same fire as when I gripped the bench in the playground. I shake my hands in front of me and something happens. I must have blinked. I shake them again — they disappear, then reappear. I shake them a third time and they go invisible for three seconds, then come back.

'Elecktra!' I shriek. 'Elecktra, my hands are invisible! I can't go to school with invisible hands!'

She is ten steps ahead. She turns slowly and sashays back to me. She flips up my eye patch, then takes my hands in hers and squeezes them tight.

'You're hurting me!' I gasp.

'Enough! Your hands are not invisible — they're right here, see?' She squeezes them again. 'You can feel this, can't you? It's just your eye patch playing tricks on you.'

I nod fervently. The eye patch — of course.

'It'd help if you walked through the gate with me,' I say, but Elecktra cuts me off.

'You know the rule!' She walks off, then yells back, 'Today of all days!'

As always, I walk the final three blocks to school alone.

THREE

Staring at Gate Two, I feel the quiver under my tongue. A torrent of thick saliva fills my mouth with the bitter taste of terror and a trickle of nervous sweat runs down my back. All the things I hate — Chinese burns, pimples, cheese, answering questions in class — are Christmas compared with having to walk through the gate to school.

I concentrate on my breathing like Mum does when she meditates. A calm spirit is the only way to stop myself puking my Hulk juice all over the outfit Elecktra's made me wear. Ever since I was little she's dressed me up like a doll. I've never worn an outfit that felt like 'me'; I always try to look like *her* and fail. I wanted to wear my own clothes today, but she said if anyone found out we were related and I was dressed as myself, then her 'social reputation' would be over.

Kids are pouring through Gate One, all dressed in casual clothes instead of our usual navy uniform. I watch Elecktra prepare to make her entrance. She hangs up her phone, bends over so her hair's hanging down and runs her hands through it to 'volumise' it, then stands and smiles with neon-white teeth. Her routine is mesmerising, if a little too practised.

Jarrod meets her at the gate. She ignores him and he follows her in. She strides in a straight line, as if walking a tightrope or a catwalk, the whole performance seeming in slow motion. It feels like the world stops for Elecktra. That's what happens when you're so pretty you look like you belong in a box. Unlike me. My messy hair isn't bright yellow like Elecktra's, but jet black, so black it's almost navy blue. I'm short for my age and have to wear glasses to see the whiteboard. Mum says it's a matter of time before I land the double whammy and get braces too.

'Roxy!' Cinnamon rests a hand on my shoulder to catch her breath. She has an energy drink in her other hand. Although her mum drops her off every morning, she gets breathless walking from the car to the gate. For casual clothes day, she is wearing baggy tracksuit pants and a loose pink kaftan. Her hair is as wild as ever, as though on fire.

'Hey! Nice tent!' Hero yells at her as he walks through Gate One.

Cinnamon tugs the bottom of her kaftan and doesn't look up. Suddenly, I see her pants wriggle.

'What's that?' I point to her right pocket, but my hand has disappeared again. I shake it, but still it's completely invisible. *It's my eye patch*, I remind myself, and stuff my hand in my pocket before Cinnamon notices anything.

'Look,' she says, her voice thick with hurt.

I peer into her pocket and two yellow eyes stare up at me.

'Cute kitten,' I say.

'Cute eye patch,' Cinnamon replies without looking up.

'Pirate chic,' I say. Two pointed black ears poke up and she smiles.

'Mum and I found him on the highway on the way to school. She said I can keep him.' Cinnamon's voice becomes light again. 'I'm going to call him Rescue.'

'How will you look after him at school?' I ask.

'He fits in my pocket, and I'll give him half my lunch. Mum thinks he's still in the back seat.' She looks down adoringly at the kitten, then surveys our surroundings. 'Don't tell,' she pleads.

'I won't,' I promise.

We both look through Gate Two. Hero and his friends have assembled at the other end of the drive. They love to start the day by taunting Gate Twoers. Hero is wearing fingerless gloves and a puffer jacket. He looks taller today, as if he's had a growth spurt. Great. Just what the world needs.

'I hate casual clothes day,' I say. 'Zigzag it?'

Cinnamon and I have a few different gateway patterns that we alternate to avoid spit bombs. The older kids like to fill straws with chewed white paper, which they spit at Gate Twoers in hard, wet darts. The paper sticks like glue in your hair and to your clothes. Spit bombs are guaranteed on casual clothes day because the bullies know kids have gone to some trouble to look good.

'What are you waiting for, Sweat Queen?' Hero yells.

Cinnamon and I break away to opposite sides of the gate. Elecktra is surrounded by her friends, but glances over at me to eye the sweat patches under my arms that are ruining her T-shirt.

'On three,' I say.

'Three!' I yell.

We run through the gate, crossing paths once then twice in a figure-eight motion. Today my feet feel light and I speed past Cinnamon. All the sugar she eats has made her slow. She's clutching at her pocket to keep the kitten safe and heaves for air as she tries to keep up with me and not spill her energy drink.

I'm too quick for the spit bombs and they miss me, speckling the path behind me, but Cinnamon cops it.

Her red afro fills with white darts, like hail on a scarlet bush. Her eyes shine with tears.

Hero and his friends laugh as we regain our composure inside the gate.

'Not here,' I tell Cinnamon and she holds back her tears. 'We'll get him back one day.'

'How? We don't have any friends here,' she says. 'We've got no backup.' Her eyes moisten again.

I take my eye patch off and fold it over her eye. 'No crying,' I say.

'Got any goggles?' Cinnamon asks, wiping a tear from her unpatched eye.

We laugh. I pick a spit bomb out of her hair. 'It's a good look — think of it as lucky fairy dust,' I say.

A heavy hand falls on Cinnamon's backpack and her unpatched eye widens as she's forcefully spun around.

'What's in your pocket?' Hero asks. His eyes are molten black. His friends encircle us. If Hero gets hold of the kitten, he'll kill it.

Cinnamon's grip tightens on her pocket and I hope the kitten has enough air to breathe. 'Nothing,' she says in a trembling voice.

'Nothing doesn't move!' Hero says.

'She's got nothing in her pocket,' I say.

His eyes shift to me without his head moving. It's a creepy way to look at people. I put a hand across

Cinnamon's chest to protect her, but my skin burns and when I look down, my hand's flashing between visible and invisible. I retract it quickly and hide it in my pocket, but it's too late. Hero's eyes are now on my pocket. Why does this invisible thing happen? Cinnamon hasn't noticed, but Hero's definitely seen something. He licks his lips. I brace for spit bombs in the eyes.

'Pizza's here!' someone yells.

Gate One kids often have pizza delivered before school and eat it in front of everyone else. The smell wafting from Gate One is tormenting. Hero glares at me for what seems like forever, then sprints off after the others.

'Saved by the smell,' I say. 'Now hide Rescue.'

Cinnamon and I take our places at the front of the geography classroom. Hero and the TCs (Too Cool kids) sprawl along the back row.

The class is hysterical. Casual clothes day makes everyone a little nuts. Despite my warning, Cinnamon still has Rescue in her pocket. He has curled up against her warm thigh and gone to sleep. He is black with white spots and under his nose he has two brown markings like a moustache.

'Who's your friend?' Hero calls out to Cinnamon, one boxing-boot heel on his desk.

Cinnamon stops breathing and her porcelain skin washes grey. She tightens her grip on her pocket.

'Your only friend!' Hero yells.

Cinnamon shuts her eyes, the way I do when I'm wishing I'm invisible.

Hero persists. 'Who's your friend?'

The class silences. Cinnamon doesn't answer.

'On ya face!' He laughs and the class joins in.

Cinnamon lets go of her pocket and leans her cheek into her hand to hide her pimple. I turn slowly to meet Hero's dark eyes. His brow pinches with a hateful thought, ready to fly at me.

Sergeant Major stomps into the classroom and everyone, even Hero, falls silent. Sergeant Major's wearing his regular uniform: commando laced-up boots, army camouflage pants and a tucked-in tight black T-shirt that seems to cut off the circulation to the bright blue veins strangling his shoulders and neck. Sergeant Major was in the war and he talks about it all the time. No one knows what war, or why everything reminds him of digging a hole and sleeping in it or slugging bullets, but it does. We went to the zoo once and saw an echidna, and he said it reminded him of the war and having to carry 'lots of stuff on his back'.

Sergeant Major is more entertaining than the other teachers, who are rusty gnomes in comparison and drone on about uniforms and rules. They all wear old people's clothes — cardigans, tweed jackets, knee-length shorts, slacks, pearls — but Sergeant Major gets away with wearing his army gear as Hindley Hall was once a boys-only school and cadets were popular.

Sergeant Major is new to Year Seven teaching. After injuring himself in the army, he said he wanted to influence new recruits. We do a lot of physical education along with geography. He says all we need to learn is where we're going and be fit enough to get there. He runs our classroom like a sleek military operation. There isn't a pen or desk out of order.

'Morning, Sergeant Major,' we chorus.

'Prepare for inspection!' Sergeant Major shouts.

We hurry, tidying our pencils, stacking our school books, straightening our belongings inside our desks, cleaning our shoes and resting them against the first right leg of our desks in a five-past-one position.

'Attention!' he orders.

Each kid snaps into a rigid position next to his or her metal-framed desk: ankles together, eyes forwards, shoulders back.

He nods in approval as he passes the first line of desks.

The classroom bin captures his attention. He stomps his right foot, rattling our desks, and strides over to the bin. He bends from his hips, with his hands in fists by his sides, to inspect its interior, then reaches in and pulls out a soft-drink can.

'Why is there an unidentified object in the bin?' he yells.

We freeze. No one owns up.

He throws the can in the recycling basket, then, on second thoughts, retrieves it. 'You know the drill!' he barks.

We do know the drill. We push our desks out in front of us by exactly half a ruler's length, sit on our hands, walk our feet out, then drop our bums to the floor, dipping our body weight from our elbows.

'One. Two. Three. Four,' Sergeant Major yells.

At ten body dips no one has owned up. My arms are beginning to burn. Cinnamon is struggling to keep her pocket to the ceiling so as not to disturb her sleeping kitten. Sergeant Major will make us all do desk squats if he discovers she's brought a pet to school.

'Nose to the plank,' Sergeant Major commands.

No one dares complain. We sit back on our chairs, pull our desks in, fold our hands behind our heads and crunch our stomachs down until our noses touch our desks, like a sit-up. Many of the kids wheeze, practically pass out, but I have always found Sergeant Major's exercises easy. I'm a natural at sport, like my mother. Our surname means 'orchid' in Japanese, but

Mum always says we live up to the meaning in English, since the Rans have always been fast. The problem is that I lack the confidence to join any of the sporting teams or even compete. I try to hide my ability from the other kids.

Dennis, a notorious soft-drink addict, is exhausted from the dips and desk crunches. He waves his white ruler and surrenders. Sergeant Major strides over to him and holds the soft-drink can at arm's length.

'Duck,' he orders.

Dennis stands under his arm and then, like a boxer, weaves to the left and right of the soft-drink can with his guard up.

'Open your books to page thirty. First one to solve the problem won't get laps,' Sergeant Major orders.

Dennis continues weaving under the can.

I notice Cinnamon wrestling with her pocket. Small beads of sweat drip from her hairline. Her bright afro swirls around her neck. Cinnamon is the most striking girl I have ever seen. If only she realised that too.

'Stop it,' I hiss.

'He wants to get out,' she whispers.

'Take him to the toilet. Let him walk around for a minute,' I whisper.

Sergeant Major doesn't notice Cinnamon slip out of class. But Hero notices. His eyes laser onto her pocket.

Dennis gives up, puts the can in the recycling basket and class begins.

'Bruce, Krew, hold up that map.' Sergeant Major indicates the rolled map leaning against the pinboard.

The boys, members of Hero's group, slouch their way to the front of the classroom. Even they don't dare to mess with Sergeant Major. They unfold the map and hold it up against the pinboard. Sergeant Major opens the top drawer of his teaching desk, takes out a handful of nuts and dried goji berries and guzzles them, then shoves his paw into his pocket. He retrieves a small staple gun and aims it at the left-hand corner of the map, still chewing, and shoots. A pin staples the map to the board and Sergeant Major shoots pins at the remaining corners.

We stare at the map of Tasmania on the board, waiting for Sergeant Major to speak.

I can feel Hero's eyes on the back of my neck. But when I turn around, he's disappeared. I can't relax.

Cinnamon slips back into the classroom with slick cheeks and swollen eyes. She takes a paintbrush from an immaculate row of bristles lined up against a pile of alphabetised folders and shoves it into Rescue's pocket, which she pats as she sits down. 'I can't find him,' she whispers in a quivering voice.

I can't risk searching for Rescue while Sergeant Major is taking class. If I get caught with the kitten, I'll get into trouble. Sergeant Major will make me run fifty laps of the oval and even though my last name is 'Ran', no one's that fit. I turn my attention to my notebook to take my mind off Rescue until after class.

Things that make me feel good, I write.

1. *Cleaning out drawers.*
2. *Spying on Lecky.*
3. *Receiving mail.*
4. *Organising my desktop.*
5. *Eavesdropping on other people's conversations, even though I know I shouldn't.*
6. *Stapling stuff.*
7. *Wrapping presents.*
8. *Cuddling hot plates from a fresh dishwasher cycle.*
9. *Checking out what books people are reading.*
10. *Cuddling pets in pet shops.*
11. *Inventing conversations between my favourite foods.*
12. *Bending paperclips into baby coathangers.*

Hero returns to class. His taunts interrupt my train of thought. 'Sweat Queen and Pimple Dimple,' Hero whispers and laughs.

Cinnamon is sobbing now. She looks so defeated, so vulnerable, that I can't wait any longer.

'I'll find Rescue,' I tell her. 'Cover for me.'

I slip out of class just as Sergeant Major switches off the lights to show us a video I am sure we've all seen before.

FOUR

Cinnamon was walking Rescue around in the toilets so that's where I begin my search. I creep down the hall, alert for teachers, and slip into the girls' toilets. I look under the bathroom stalls, behind the sinks, out the window — but no Rescue. I call his name quietly, but I don't think he's even had a chance to learn it yet.

'Kitty Kat! Kit Kit? Little Puss! Rescue?' I whisper, but nothing.

I am feeling light-headed and put it down to the stress of casual clothes day. My body is unusually hot, the hair at the base of my ponytail wet. My heart is racing and I feel like I'm getting sick.

The boys' and girls' toilets are located in one large fluorescent-lit room with a high dividing wall between them. There's a narrow space at the base of the wall, just big enough for a kitten to crawl through. The boys try to use the space as a spy hole. I crouch down, nose to the tiles, but I can't see the kitten.

A pair of boxing boots enters the boys' toilets. There's a rustling sound, then the opening of a cubicle door, then I hear a noise that drains the blood from my face. A tiny mew.

'Rescue!'

I leap to my feet and throw myself towards the top of the dividing wall. I misjudge the distance and hit my head on the roof as I go over, and smash to the ground. I expect to feel Hero's boot in my cheek, but when I stand, he has his back to me. I look in disbelief over my shoulder at the wall. It's twice my height and yet I leaped over it!

I look down at my torso and hands: they're invisible. My skinny jeans and ballet flats are standing here all on their own.

Hero turns slowly and I see that he's holding Rescue's tiny black and white body over the toilet bowl by the scruff of the kitten's neck. His other hand's resting on the flush button.

'I know it's you,' he says, even though he can't see my face. 'Don't come any closer or I'll flush it!'

His eyes flicker furiously as he tries to see me. He seems unperturbed that half of my body is invisible. Serrated black clouds move across the whites of his eyes. His hair becomes hard like stone and his skin turns the colour of rock.

'Let go of him and I won't tell,' I say.

As soon as I speak, my arms and torso become visible again. Hero smiles evilly.

'I knew it was you,' he says.

'What do you mean?' I say. I try to sound tough, but my voice squeaks.

'I hate ferrets,' he says and drops the kitten into the toilet bowl. Rescue squeals.

The same fire I felt on the bench in the playground returns and swells in my ankles. I feel it burn up into my kneecaps. Before I can bring it under control, I am propelling myself towards Hero. I knee him in the back of his knee and land with my feet either side of the toilet bowl. Rescue is drowning. I swoop to pick him up, but Hero grabs my hand and yanks it backwards, throwing my body out of the cubicle and crashing it against the toilet wall. Rescue flies out of my hand and plunges back into the toilet. Hero barricades the cubicle and reaches for the flush.

Soaring to my feet, I sprint towards him; it feels as though my feet are coated in oil, gliding across the tiles before take-off. I launch into the air and my left leg stretches out, my right leg bends underneath in support and my hands punch out in straight arms, arrowing towards Hero's jaw. I tell my body to relax. I strike and watch in disbelief as Hero's jaw slams into the side of the cubicle. Part of me wants to apologise and run, but Rescue is still floundering in the toilet bowl, his eyes closed, pawing at the dirty water. With wet fur he has shrunk. I race to pluck him out, but Hero sweeps my leg from under me, arm-bars my right arm, locks my wrist and slowly, excruciatingly, bends my arm back towards his chest. We watch Rescue fight for his life in the deathly suck of the flush, his legs tiring as they struggle to keep his head above the water.

'I know what you are,' Hero whispers in his cruel voice. 'And since you don't, the kitten will die.'

The fire rushes out of my body and I become very still. I squeeze my fists. *What is going on?* My heart is a hammer, my fingertips tingling, I'm freaking out at my sudden ability.

Then Hero's friends walk in and snap me out of it. Now there are three boys surrounding me. Bruce isn't that tall, but he's the fastest kid in school, with knuckles as large as knees; and Krew has a similar vibe to a brick wall: flat and impassable. Hero releases the arm bar and locks both my arms by my side, then leans in from behind me and smells my neck.

'I know who you are,' he sneers.

Hero holds me in place while Bruce pushes me hard. My neck jars and my skin smoulders. 'That's just for thinking you're better than everyone,' Bruce says.

His short, curly brown hair is gelled close to his head like a helmet. I reckon if I punch it, I'll hurt my hand. I look at Rescue: the flush has stopped and he's still treading water.

'Why do you hate me so much?' I say in a strangled voice.

'Ask your mum.' Hero's sour breath congeals on my neck.

I turn my chin away from him. Why does he keep taunting me about my parents?

'Your mum's boyfriend's an unemployed loser,' Krew says.

'Yeah,' Hero says, 'they're a pair of hippies.'

All of a sudden, I am aware of my every heartbeat. My chest rises with a single tidal breath to give wind to my next move. I slam my hips back into Hero's groin, simultaneously snapping my hands forwards to break his grip. He crouches over his groin as I knife my front heel into Bruce's groin at the same moment that he kicks out towards me. The power of my strike propels him backwards into the sinks. He cracks against the porcelain and falls to the floor.

With one leap I am at the toilet bowl and lifting the drowning kitten out of the water. Rescue collapses on the palm of my hand; I can feel his thimble-sized heart raging. He opens his eyes and coughs. I place him on the floor beside the toilet as Bruce and Krew step into the cubicle either side of me. I don't know where my powers have come from, but I'm happy to test them out on these two.

We barely fit in the cramped space, so I snap my leg up past my right shoulder and spear Krew across the collarbone. My muscles and tendons are totally flexible for the first time in my life and feel like elastic bands that snap and whip. Bruce has an iron grip on my arm. I swing my left leg over his arm, slash his knee with my toes, then kick over his arm again to cane his other knee with a flick of my hamstring. I smile. You gotta make it even!

He looks at me in pain and confusion, before I move the sole of my foot to his face and lean my weight backwards. I wait for him to heave me forwards, and when he does, somehow I know to absorb his force into my foot and strike it into his nose. His eyes burst with tears.

Hero picks up Rescue and tosses him back into the toilet bowl. He turns to me, striking outwards with supernatural strength, but he is no match for my new techniques. I catch his fist between both my hands, stamp my heel hard on his shoulder socket, then slide into the same pain-gripping arm bar that he used to hold me hostage before.

The door to the toilet block slams open. I release Hero. Bruce and Krew scuttle to the urinals and I lean casually against the wall as if nothing is happening. Dennis walks in.

'You're not allowed in here!' he says to me.

Hero leans over me as if he's about to kiss me.

'Oh, sorry, Hero,' Dennis says and leaves.

Hero grabs my hair from the front. I feel the roots bite my skull to stay attached. As his grip tightens, I almost scream. But again, I know instinctively what to do. I slap both my hands down across his knuckles, flattening them against my crown, then I step back, twist my body and, with a firm grip on his arm, twirl his entire body in the air without releasing my grip on his knuckles, then let him go to fall hard on his back.

I race for the kitten, but Hero is too quick. He flushes the toilet again and this time Rescue is struggling harder to stay out of the vacuum of water.

'Nooo!' I yell. Tears stand in my eyes as the three boys approach. There is no time to save him.

I crouch into a low fighting form and study Hero with tigerish eyes. I feel my muscles, reflexes, speed awakening. I kick off my shoes to feel more balanced. I've never kicked with my bare feet before and hope the birthmark on my right sole will freak out the boys.

Hero's eyes fire a message to his friends: he wants to take me out himself. I feel a prickling on my skin, as if someone else is in here, watching, but there is no time to turn and look.

When Hero launches for my throat, an innate sense of knowing envelops me; a mixture of skill and technique flames into my muscle fibres stronger than memory — instinct. As soon as his fingers clamp around my neck, I reach my knee between us and kick his nose. He sees the birthmark on my foot and gasps. He stutters something, but I don't hear him. I slam the blades of my hands into his elbows to weaken his grip and pull him closer. 'Slow learner, aren't you?' I say.

With his hands still clutching my neck, I blast the pressure points in his upper arms with short, sharp strikes, lashing out with my elbows, wrists and hands, then knee him in the groin. When I am staring deep into his dark eyes, certain that he tastes the bile of fear dripping from his tonsils, I arch my neck backwards, tempted to spit in his eyes, but am glad I don't sink to his level.

I scoop up Rescue and race over to the hand dryer to warm him. He coughs up water. Bruce and Krew have backed off; they're watching Hero doubled over on the floor. I don't know what just happened, but whatever it was, it felt awesome!

As I walk out into the corridor with Rescue in my pocket, a hand grabs my right shoulder from behind. I turn sharply, lift my arm to brush the hand off my shoulder and scoop it into an instant arm lock. A pair of speckled green eyes shimmering with shavings of gold stares down at me from beneath a backward cap. It's as if I'm being seen for the first time ever. I release my grip.

Green Eyes straightens himself up and smiles. 'Fast,' he says, then winks.

I dissolve into a blush and cast my eyes down. When I look up, the boy has disappeared and the corridor feels cold and empty.

FIVE

'There you are!' I clutch Cinnamon's arm. 'We've got PE in the gym now and Sergeant Major will turn troll if we're late! Where've you been?'

'Looking for you,' she says.

'Rescue's safe in your locker,' I say.

Beaming, Cinnamon grabs my hand and hurries us to her locker to check on him. Rescue is fast asleep, recovering from his mammoth swim. I don't tell Cim about his near-death experience.

In the gym, Sergeant Major has gone to collect a visitor and left Year Seven unattended. Kids are climbing the ladders on the walls, throwing balls and brick-sized beanbags at each other, wrestling on the mats and screaming. Whenever a teacher leaves a group of kids alone, their natural reaction is to scream their lungs out — any kid will tell you that.

'Want to go on a date?' Krew calls to Cinnamon. He doesn't make eye contact with me.

Cinnamon's eyes brighten.

'To a fat camp!' He laughs.

Cinnamon's eyes fill with tears. I grab her arm. She bites her lip and the tears seep away. She's had good practice at swallowing sadness.

'Hey, wanna come over later and play with Rescue?' she asks. 'We could hang out together and check out some clothes online?'

Cinnamon loves to trawl through dresses on the internet. She never wears dresses because they often don't fit her. But online she can pretend to shop at all our favourite stores.

I think Cinnamon is beautiful the way she is, but I know every time a boy calls her 'Cinnamon donut' she eats more and then hates herself for it. I've tried to tell her they are only words, but she says the food makes the words go away. I guess she'd rather feel full than hurt.

'I'd love to come,' I say. 'I'll head over after school.'

Cinnamon's smile leaps towards the light. 'We can go visit my horse too,' she says.

'Really?' I say.

Cinnamon's face blushes with pain. 'I don't ride any more, but you can,' she says. She hesitates, then finally mumbles, 'It's not fair on him.'

Her forlorn face fractures my heart. 'Cinnamon, I can help you onto him. What's his name again?'

'Elf.' She nods.

There is a long pause licked with tears about to burst. Cinnamon's fingers are knotted like lace.

'How long since you've ridden Elf?' I ask.

'Six months,' she says, looking away. 'But,' she pauses, 'maybe if I had a friend with me ...' She looks back at me hopefully.

I've tried to help Cinnamon, trading my lunch with hers, telling her the secret recipe to Hulk juice, showing her some of my mum's moves, but she never sticks to it. It's like she lets the stuff the kids say crawl deep down and then feeds those feelings with food. 'I'll come and see Elf with you after school,' I say.

'Promise?' she asks, holding out her pinkie finger.

'What are we, Year Three?' I say.

'Okay, spit swear,' she says. We spit in our hands and shake on it.

I am swinging from the gymnastic rings when Sergeant Major explodes through the door with another man also dressed in camouflage pants, but instead of a black T-shirt like Sergeant Major's, he's wearing a camouflage jacket and matching camo cap.

'Attention!' Sergeant Major booms. 'I didn't give up the army to teach Year Seven and have them behave like hooligans.'

We stop screaming and instantly fall into side-by-side line formation, each kid's left hand outstretched to the next kid's shoulder.

'I could have done anything after my Service, but I chose to teach Year Seven. Year Two — too distracted!' he yells. 'Year Three — still too distracted. Years Four,' he pauses to inspect the distance between one kid's fingers and the next person's shoulder and adjusts them to be closer, 'and Five — too slow and Year Six all that i-stuff kicks in,' he huffs. 'I say, give me Year Seven. Impressionable. Smart. Fast. Resilient. Don't make me change my mind.

'Eyes front,' Sergeant Major orders and we snap our heads to look at him. 'This here,' he slaps the man standing next to him on the back, 'is Private Lincoln.'

Private Lincoln stamps his right foot and salutes Sergeant Major.

'Private Lincoln is in the army,' Sergeant Major barks, 'and he's come here today to teach you about Stranger Danger.'

Sergeant Major is called away by the school PA system to take an urgent phone call. We are left staring at only the second soldier we have ever seen in our lives.

'Sit,' Private Lincoln commands.

We all plummet to the floor and sit cross-legged. Joshua is the last one down.

'Pay attention!' Private Lincoln commands.

Josh crosses his legs. We sit up even straighter.

'What do you do if a stranger in a van pulls up as you're walking to school and offers you a bag of sweets?' he asks. 'Would you get in the vehicle?'

We are too nervous to answer.

'Hands up!' he yells.

The whole class shoots both their hands in the air as if surrendering to a gunman.

'Yes.' He points at Martin.

'Nope,' Martin says in an uncertain voice.

'Tick!' Private Lincoln yells. 'What would you do if the stranger in the van offered you a Nintendo?'

'What sort of Nintendo?' Gregory asks.

'DS.'

'Nah, already got one,' Gregory says.

'Tick,' Private Lincoln says, a smile in his voice. 'What about a Wii?'

'That too!' Gregory yells.

'The latest iPad?'

'Get in!' we chorus.

Private Lincoln's face clouds over. 'No!' he shouts. 'Tick, tick, cross. Don't move,' he barks and disappears.

As soon as he leaves the room, the natural instinct to go wild takes over again and we run around yelling and giggling, swinging and throwing and laughing, until we hear footsteps and line up again.

Private Lincoln enters the gym wearing a fat suit. His head with its camouflage cap pokes out of the top; it looks tiny perched on the suit's dinghy-sized shoulders. The legs are like two inflatable swimming pools, making it hard for him to walk. He waddles to the front of our line. Across his chest is a massive bulletproof jacket and he's wearing a fluorescent green mouthguard. I know from school sports, only serious people choose fluorescent mouthguards. If you're not serious, you go with clear.

'One at a time, you're going to attack me!' Private Lincoln shouts. 'I want you to kick me with all your strength. When I fall down, you go to the back of the line. But you must make me fall down.'

Hero cracks his knuckles and I suddenly feel sorry for Private Lincoln.

My hands begin to sweat. I've never attacked anyone before ... except for a few minutes ago in the boys' toilets. And I still can't believe I did that! I don't know what's come over me lately. I've already lost control once today and I'm terrified what might happen if I strike out again.

'Psst,' someone says behind me.

I whip my head around to see the mysterious boy with the grass-green eyes slipping into the line next to me.

'What are you doing here?' I say out of the corner of my mouth so Private Lincoln doesn't notice.

'I go to school here now, in Year Ten. I need to talk to you.'

'Not now,' I whisper. 'I'm about to take on a man in a fat suit.'

'Come with me,' he says, grabbing me by the wrist.

'YOU!' Private Lincoln thunders. My heart stops. He's pointing at me. He turns his index finger to the roof and wiggles it, summoning me to him.

I step forwards.

'No!' he yells. 'Not you, you!'

The boy with emerald eyes steps out from beside me.

'Front and centre,' Private Lincoln orders, and the boy walks hesitantly to the front.

I notice Hero's eyes flash with rage — and recognition. Does he know this boy? From his last school maybe?

'Since you have so much to say, you can go first,' Private Lincoln tells the boy. 'Show everyone how it's done.'

The boy's shoulders slouch and he looks at the floor. He must be terrified. Fair enough. I feel sorry for him. He's going to get pummelled in his first week at school and it's all my fault.

'Ready ready?' Private Lincoln shouts.

The boy doesn't move.

Private Lincoln launches at him with his arms in the air and for a second the boy is completely enveloped in the fat suit. I gasp. Then the soldier's arms fly backwards as the boy leaps up level with his shoulders and double-knees him playfully in the chest. He rebounds off the suit, spins once, extending his back leg like a scorpion, then his supporting leg shoots into the air and he hits Private Lincoln in the right shoulder, knocking him sideways. Private Lincoln teeters for a moment, before the boy jumps in the air again, forceps the soldier's neck between his ankles and flips his body over his head. Private Lincoln lands on his back and the boy leaps onto his stomach and takes a slight bow. The class cheers.

'Cease and desist,' Private Lincoln commands, still on his back. He's unable to stand in the fat suit.

But the boy ignores him and continues to play to the crowd. We cheer louder and louder until Sergeant Major storms into the gym and pulls the boy off Private Lincoln by the scruff of his neck. Private Lincoln stands up and takes his position at the front of the line again.

'Next,' he says and points to me with a wiggling finger. I approach him with a turtle shuffle.

'Ready?' he says, and I dive for his shoelaces, yank them upwards and send him rolling onto his back again.

Then I drive my shoe into his private parts, imagining he's a stranger about to mug or kidnap me.

The class silences. They haven't seen this side of me before — although I'm not sure if they know *any* side of me, possibly even my name. But since rescuing Rescue in the boys' toilets, I'm imbued with a confidence that hardens me against whatever the class may think.

'Cease and desist!' Private Lincoln yells in a high-pitched voice.

Sergeant Major, still holding Green Eyes by the scruff of his neck, launches at me with his other hand and catches me by the back of my T-shirt. Holding on tight, he leads us away. I swallow hard. I've never been in trouble before. Ever. I suddenly regret even coming to school this morning.

'Beating up Private Lincoln was not the point of the exercise,' Sergeant Major growls. 'Self-control is the path between where you are and where you should be.'

I am too embarrassed to look at Green Eyes, but I notice every girl's eyes on me as we're led away together. I'm guessing they are wishing it was them being hauled off to detention with him, instead of me. Most of them haven't had the chance to meet him yet and flick their hair, hoping he'll notice.

Sergeant Major drops us near the equipment cupboard in the far corner of the gym and tells us to 'Stay'. Even

Green Eyes doesn't dare disobey him and we sit there in silence until the class finishes, the gym empties and all that's left of Stranger Danger is Private Lincoln's fat suit hanging over a ladder stapled to the wall.

In all that time, Green Eyes and I haven't said a word to each other. He's found a clipboard with paper and is drawing. I'm biting my nails. Being this close to those forest eyes, the blond hair sweeping over his face, the strong shoulders and sharp jaw, is giving me goose bumps. I'm tongue-tied; deciding whether or not to speak to him is like wringing out a towel in my mouth.

I clear my throat. He doesn't look up.

I stand up and move closer. 'Um …' I watch his hand caress the paper. 'What are you drawing?'

He looks up and his eyes glow against the dark walls.

'See.' He smiles and lifts the page to show me two words embossed with what look like stars.

'Looks good. What does it say?'

The boy's smile is peanut-butter thick. 'Thanks, Fancy Face. It says "White Warrior".'

'What's that?'

He doesn't answer, just puts the clipboard down, slides his elbows onto his knees and rests his head on his hand. I sit back down on a pile of crash mats. I look around the room, trying to think of something else to talk about, but I have to ask.

'What do you mean by "fancy"?'

He hasn't taken his eyes off me. 'Well ... pretty,' he says gently.

I drop my head, wishing I knew what to say.

He continues. 'But you'd get told that all the time.'

I shake my head violently and my eye patch comes loose. Damn, I forgot I was wearing that stupid thing. Here I am with the cutest boy in school and I'm wearing a pirate patch. Lame! Then I realise I haven't answered him.

'Never,' I say.

'The world needs glasses,' he says, leaning back and folding his arms behind his head. 'And braces.'

'Braces?'

'Must be bent if it doesn't think you're pretty,' he says.

I smile and feel my entire being blush.

'Why are you saying this to me? I don't even know you.'

'I know you.' He points at me. 'You've shown a lot of yourself today.'

I look at him, confused.

'The boys' toilets? Saving the cat?'

I gasp. 'You were there?'

'I was in the next cubicle.' He laughs.

'I didn't mean to hurt anyone. I don't know what's going on with me lately.' I tie my fingers up in knots and unpick them, not looking at him.

'Midteen crisis?' he offers.

'What?'

'Just joking. It's not a midteen crisis. I know what's going on with you and I'm going to need your help.' He stands at the sound of footsteps — Sergeant Major coming to dismiss us. 'I'm Jackson Axe, by the way.'

'I'm Roxy. Roxy Ran, and why do you need my help?'

He picks up his 'White Warrior' drawing and taps the page. 'I need to find this,' he says. 'And you can help me. Meet me after lunch at Gate One.'

I nod quickly before the door opens and Sergeant Major barges into the gym. We head out to lunch.

SIX

I'm on my way to Gate One to meet Jackson as planned. I'm very early, but I'm too scared of missing him to wait in the library.

'Roxy!'

I recognise my sister's voice. Can't I wag school in peace?

I spin around and Elecktra glares at me. 'Where are you going?' she asks.

If angel honey existed, it would be the exact colour of Elecktra's hair glistening in the sun.

'I-I,' I stutter, looking around for Jackson to save me. But I'm early so he's nowhere in sight.

Elecktra grabs my wrist and throws my arm up in the air. 'How many times do I have to tell you to stop sweating on my clothes?' she whines. 'It's hideous!'

Suddenly, a gaggle of her girlfriends is surrounding us, including Chantell Best, who's in Year Seven but cool enough to hang out with the older girls. She is the worst of Lecky's clique, the only girl I know who tries to calm herself with one of her mother's lattes.

'She should wear better deodorant to stop the sweat,' Chantell says. She's wearing a ribbon around her head, like she's an Easter egg.

'I do wear deodorant,' I say.

'Could've fooled me.' Chantell loves to bicker.

'I'm sick of this,' Elecktra says. 'I lend you my top and you get stains all over it. I don't know why I bother.'

'Why'd you lend a Gate Two your top anyway?' Chantell asks.

'She begged me,' Elecktra says quietly.

My heart blooms with burrs. I stare at the freckle on Elecktra's chin; I have one exactly the same and we used to pretend we were twins. A stone sinks in my throat and I have to look away. I stare at Gate One in the distance.

'Elecktra, is that a croissant?' Chantell asks, pointing to the chocolate croissant Elecktra holds in her hand. Elecktra tears off the corner with her teeth.

'OMGOMG, I would totally need an occasion to eat that,' Chantell says. Elecktra swallows and ignores her.

'Take it off,' Elecktra demands.

The girls clap their palms without touching fingers so as not to ruin their manicures. I keep my eyes focused on the school gate. The iron bars no longer signify any hope of social networking or party invites; they feel prison-like. I turn back to Elecktra.

'But I've only got a crop top on underneath,' I whisper.

'A crop top!' Elecktra says at the top of her voice.

My cheeks sting.

'Hand it over,' she says. 'ASAP!'

I know she's stubborn and won't let up. More kids wander over, drawn by her shouting. She holds out her hand. 'Give it to me,' she says.

I've never wagged school before, but I know stripping down before you do isn't the best way to slip past the teachers unnoticed. But those green eyes are inked on my brain, haunting, coaxing. I have no choice and wonder yet again if she really is my sister.

I slam my backpack down and rip off Elecktra's T-shirt, revealing my sports crop top underneath. 'Happy?' I say.

Her girlfriends erupt into laughter as I run towards the gate without looking back. Elecktra chases after me, but I'm too quick for her. All that sugar she's sneaking has slowed her down.

'You can't just leave!' she calls. 'I'll tell!'

I sprint faster and block out the sound of her voice. I get the same feeling of freedom as when I leaped over the toilet wall and gave Hero a serve.

'You can't leave through Gate One!' Elecktra yells as I run through it. 'You're not authorised!'

Instead of waiting to meet Jackson, I race home. It's all been too much — my invisible hands and torso, the fight with Hero, the awful things he said about me and my family.

When I arrive at our yellow warehouse, no one's home. I collapse at the kitchen table, sobbing over the old boat planks. My tears darken the wood.

I smooth my hand across the table. I love this surface — it's like me: fragmented, forced to fit in with different kinds of wood even though they're all different. I wish I could rebuild the planks into a boat and cast off onto the ocean, away from all this confusion.

I get a tea towel and dab at the wood, cleaning away my tears. But the wood has already soaked them up. This table has soaked up so much of our lives over the years.

I think again about what Hero said about my parents. His words have been sitting undigested in my gut for hours, like gum. His use of 'fatherless' the other day is still an alarm in my heart. Hero knows something and that gives him power over me. I can't ask Mum about it. So while Mum's at work and Art is out somewhere, probably buying paint, I decide to search.

I start in Mum and Art's bedroom. The double bed is made with martial precision; I imagine Mum practising her strikes to tuck in the corners of the sheets. The bedside tables are low industrial filing cabinets with white domed lamps. I check inside. Mum's is empty. Art's is full of throat lozenges. Their walk-in wardrobe is just as disappointing. Mum's side is all colour coordinated; even her gym lycra is neatly folded. Art's side is a mess, with paint-stained jeans and speckled boots strewn over piles of the flannel shirts he buys at the supermarket. There is no sign of ninja, of my father, of any secrets. I hoist myself up to the top shelf, but again, nothing. Not even Mum's black belt. Everything to do with what she calls her 'past life' has been either hidden or destroyed — except for the knives that she uses in the kitchen. They serve a practical purpose, whereas the rest, Mum says, is sentimental, and as a ninja she can't afford to indulge in sentimentality.

I wish we had a study with a safe I could crack. But we don't. I think half the reason we live in an open-plan warehouse apartment is so nothing can be hidden away. Our house is secret-proof.

Downstairs, I don't bother with the kitchen or the living room, but go straight to the antique cabinet that houses the photo albums. I still have a fantasy that one day I'll stumble across an old, curled, yellowing photo of my father holding me. I'll keep it in my school diary and show people, saying, 'He was a great man. A legend.'

Maybe I'd even tell them I was now an orphan to up the sympathy.

The cabinet smells of the bush — eucalyptus. I open the glass doors. The photo albums are numbered by year. I take out 2000 and flick through the pages. I am one year old and Elecktra is four. Elecktra has a bowl haircut, buckteeth and a big nose. I open 2007: Elecktra is eleven and has grown into her nose, but she's wearing braces. One year later and the photos reveal her battle with chronic acne. Who knew Lecky used to be ugly? I slide out a photo of her in the full get-up: the braces, acne and a square fringe that's thicker than the rest of her hair. It is the worst photo I've ever seen of her. I put it into my pocket for insurance.

I search the rest of the photo albums, but they only feature Mum, Art, Lecky, me and a few random friends of my parents, like Art's German mate, Hacky, who's a sculptor.

Sometimes when I look at Lecky now, with her flawless skin and fountain of blonde hair, or watch Mum's superb knife skills, I feel like I don't belong in this family, like I got kicked out of the gene pool to wade in a weak puddle. My heart sinks. I know the reason I feel so different, the reason why bits and pieces of me have been flashing invisible all week, has something to do with my mother, and I'm somehow going to have to find out what it is.

SEVEN

I hurry back to school and arrive just in time to meet Jackson on the street near Gate One.

'Hey, Roxy!' he calls.

As he jogs towards me, he grabs the bottom of his hoodie and lifts it over his head. I watch him wrestle with the arms and as he approaches he hands it to me. 'Go on. You look cold.'

I'd put another T-shirt on at home, but take his hoodie anyway. It smells comforting, a mix of washing powder and hot pasta sauce.

'You ready, Fancy Face?' he asks and turns to leave. I love it when he calls me that.

'Wait,' I say.

He spins back around, his blond hair whipping his forehead. I blink myself out of the slow-motion picture I keep seeing whenever he moves.

'Hang on a minute,' I say. 'I need to take a picture and send it to someone.'

'Sure,' he says. It takes two minutes to rephotograph the photo of Elecktra and send it to her. Jackson stretches as he waits.

'Done,' I say as I pocket my phone.

We set out at a pace that ordinarily I would struggle to maintain, but today I'm too fast and Jackson has to tell me to slow down.

We go to Becker Hill Parade, to a school about twenty minutes from Hindley Hall. A group of kids dressed in white martial arts uniforms is standing next to a trailer.

'Who are they?' I ask.

'My Taekwondo instructor's demo team,' Jackson says. 'They're here for the school open day.'

'Demo?'

'Entertainment,' he says and signals me to follow him.

The huge trailer is parked at the back of the school oval. You couldn't miss it. A life-sized photo of a man doing a front kick stretches from the trailer's tyres to the top of its steel cabin. Across his billowing stomach are the words *Discipline. Focus. Fun.* painted in primary colours. A trestle table with only three good legs wobbles beside the trailer; on it is a pinboard of photos showing kids doing a range of martial arts moves and a signing-up list for classes.

Jackson takes me inside the trailer, where the demo team is now circled up among kick pads, mats and sandwich-board signs. Their uniforms look a bit more grey than white and a recent outdoor demo has stamped red Vs on the exposed skin of their chests.

'Who's the king of the demo?' a man in his fifties calls. He is wearing the white uniform too, with a black belt with four stripes.

'You are, sir, Sabomin, sir!' the team yells in unison.

Jackson tells me 'Sabomin' is the Korean word for 'teacher', but the students call him 'Sabo' for short.

'Hands in,' Sabo says.

They all put their hands in the circle.

'It's showtime, team. This is what it's all about. Performing for the people. You're only as good as your what?'

'Last demo,' they chorus.

'Let's go over the plan. Ed will kick things off with a pattern — get them hook, line and sinker. Then I'll step in and seal the deal. Salvatore, you holding my board?'

'Yes, Sabomin,' Salvatore says.

'Okay, Ed, get kicking. Sally, balloons. Kellie, play it cool. Salvatore, tell the audience ten minutes until showtime. This is a big demo for us. Let's really Glee it up!' Sabomin blows his whistle twice, then yells, *'Kiyap!'*

The team punch their fists forwards from their chests, stomp and yell, 'Ay-yah!', before spilling out of the trailer onto the school oval.

I guess it must be an ordinary kind of open day: there's a sagging jumping castle with a sprinkling of children collapsing into its folds, a few stalls selling handmade lipstick cases and tea cosies, and a sausage sizzle to raise money for the school library. Kids congregate in packs away from their parents, who stand around chatting while they wait to tour the school. The school buildings around us are the same colour as the grey asphalt; they shiver in the shade. The cindery dust of the oval clouds my eyes.

Sabomin presses Play on the stereo and thumping music mangles out through the metal casing.

Ed takes his place at the centre of the oval and begins his pattern. I see how he concentrates on his technical precision, angling his eye line with the degree of his kick, twisting through his hip on his body blocks to create extra snap in his uniform, and flicking his wrist so that his knife hands sound like whips.

A kid approaches with his parents. Despite Salvatore's coaxing, they refuse to stand where he suggests and instead watch from afar with all the enthusiasm of waiting in a queue at a supermarket checkout.

'One, two,' Ed says under his breath, tucking his knee into his hip and snapping the blade of his foot above his ear in a double side kick. I would give anything to be able to do that. He breathes through the movements, measuring his steps so that he finishes in the exact same position as he started.

'I've never seen anything like this,' I say to Jackson.

Jackson blazes his green eyes towards me and smiles proudly.

'My favourite-ever demos Sabomin's done are one: the Island Cheese Company "Cheese is our life" convention, on a floating barge on a river; two: Petra Peters Real Estate; three: a sixth birthday party at FunCity; four: a performance for a top athlete, who loves Taekwondo and bumped into Sabo at the Olympics. Sabo had to drop everything and demo on the spot. Five: Mega Eyewear for "Eye Love Sunglasses" day. Plus, Sabo won an award,' Jackson pauses casually, 'when we did a demo at the Royal Easter Show in 2006: third-best display in the Sports and Leisure Pavilion.'

'Impressive,' I say and nod at Ed. 'Can you do that?'

'Practising on your own exercises the mind and teaches you focus,' Jackson says to me.

When he leans in close, the smell of him creates a kind of energy. I pretend to check out my nails like I've seen Elecktra do whenever someone is trying to explain something to her. I also try to ignore the fact that I'm wearing his hoodie and can't escape his smell even if I wanted to.

Sabomin's voice pulls me back to the demo. Ed finishes and bows deeply ... to no applause, even though Salvatore's managed to drag a group of teenaged boys over to form a small audience.

'When's he going to smash someone?' one boy yells.

Sabomin takes Ed's place on the oval. Salvatore and Kellie run out with an armful each of tiles and stack them on two blocks. Sabomin rolls a shin guard over his uniform and throws his whistle to the side with a dramatic open hand.

'To bust tiles with your elbow is one of the most difficult things to do in Taekwondo,' he says. 'I consider myself a master in this.'

Sabomin lowers his elbow to the tiles to achieve the correct position. He does it again, gritting his teeth, his breathing in sync with his movement. He signals Salvatore to cut the music.

'*Hannah. Dul. Set,*' he counts in Korean, then slams his elbow into the centre of the tiles with an 'Ay-yaaayaya-yah!'

The tiles crack with the weak sound of a window popping open. There are feeble claps from the audience.

Sabomin turns to his team, who are leaning against the trailer, watching the master at work. 'Damn,' he says and shakes his arm out.

He turns back to the spectators. 'They were tiles, people. Tiles!'

A sip of coffee, checking of a phone; nobody really cares.

Salvatore appears with a square piece of pine wood and holds it out towards Sabomin's head. His fingers grip the bottom of the board. Sabomin bows to the piece of wood.

'*Hannah. Dul. Set!*' he yells, then rushes at the board with the heel of his palm.

Instead of snapping into pieces, the board flies out of Salvatore's hand and lands intact on its side, rolling in a circle like a coin before tipping to the ground.

'Stunt double!' Sabomin calls. He points to me.

I look at Jackson.

'Don't be shy,' he says.

I pick up the board and hand it to Salvatore. Is this what Mum means by getting your ninja on? Usually I wouldn't have the confidence even to stand up in front of a crowd and now I've walked out and committed myself to breaking wood with my limbs. I must be mad!

Salvatore holds the plank of wood above his head between his outstretched arms. I've never done this before, but that feeling of instinct returns and, without counting to three, without thinking, I jump into a climbing double front kick and snap the board into three pieces. Two of them fly so high into the sky they seem to disappear. The third bit of wood almost hits a pram. The mother kicks off the brake, spins the pram violently and steers her child back towards the jumping castle, which is now so deflated the kids are touching concrete on every bounce.

'If anyone wants to sign up for classes, please come talk to me. I run boot camps too,' Sabomin says to the three people left watching. They are arching their heads to the sky, still searching for those pieces of wood.

'Do you do yoga classes?' a mother asks, clutching her empty coffee cup. I'd seen her look of horror as she refused the instant coffee being handed out by the parents' committee.

'As a former champion,' Sabomin says, placing his hands on his hips, 'I know how important it is to have mind control. Meditation is a big part of any martial artist's life.' He pauses and smooths his hand down his chest to soothe his heartburn, then burps in his throat and excuses himself. 'But has yoga ever saved anyone's life?' he says, staring the woman right in the eye.

The woman holds his stare then leaves, shaking her head.

'Roxy, wait here to sign people up. I've got to find the school principal,' Sabomin says.

'But I don't ... How do you know my name, Sabomin?'

'I've had an idea,' he says, ignoring my question. 'And call me Sabo.' Then he asks, 'Heard of a swagger coach?'

I shake my head.

'The team needs a bit more swagger, more polish. All the US hip-hop artists use them, you know?' He taps a finger on his chin, which is covered in stubble that shines grey in the sun. 'Leave it with me,' he says and hurries off.

Jackson is talking to other members of the team, so I walk over to the trestle table to look at the demo photos. Salvatore is there too, talking to a kid he's managed to get to take a flyer.

'Taekwondo's the best,' Salvatore says.

'Taekwondo's lame,' the kid argues. 'All that protective gear you fight in. You don't punch in the face.'

'Why punch in the face when you can kick in the face?' Salvatore says.

'Taekwondo copied Karate,' the boy says.

'Not possible. Karate is Japanese.'

'So?' the boy says.

'Taekwondo is Korean,' Salvatore says, taking back the flyer he just handed the boy. Obviously, he doesn't think he deserves one after those comments.

The sound of a skateboard roars towards us and I turn just in time to see Hero skid to a stop in front of me. He's holding a monster green slurpee in his right hand. He grabs a handful of flyers, throws them on the ground and rolls his skateboard back and forth over them.

Everything seems to sag around me: the sausages slip out of their bread at the sausage sizzle, the jumping castle collapses in on itself, the trestle tables droop with the weight of leftover fundraiser carrot cakes. How did Hero know I was here? I clench my teeth. Has he told anyone about me skipping school?

'So, you've made friends with him?' He points to Jackson, then runs a finger over a picture of Sabomin posing with somebody dressed up in an Easter Bunny suit. 'These guys are real scary,' he jeers. He rips a pin from the corner of the board and stabs it through every person's eyes on the A3 laminated team photo. I launch at him, but he steps back and chucks his chlorine-coloured slurpee at me — just as Sabomin steps between us. In an instant, Sabomin's pristine white uniform flashes snot green.

'This little display of yours is a waste of time,' Hero sneers at Sabomin. 'I'll find him first.'

'What are you talking about?' I ask.

'Stop pretending,' Hero sneers. 'You're a liar, just like your mother.'

I can't believe he said that! I clench my fists, but before I can react, he's roared off on his skateboard.

Sabomin puts a hand on my shoulder and examines the vandalised photo of the demo team. Their pricked-out eyes make them all look like ghosts in their white uniforms.

'Sure hope you didn't sign that kid up,' he says.

'I'm so sorry,' I say, looking at the slurpee dripping from his uniform.

'It'll wash out.' He smiles. 'The problem is his, not mine. It's an important life lesson to learn.'

Jackson comes over. 'Was that Hero?' he says, looking at Sabomin's uniform.

'How do you know him?' I ask.

'We used to go to the same martial arts school,' Jackson says. 'Now we compete against each other in comp.'

'And who is he talking about?'

Jackson's eyebrows thread together in frustration. 'The White Warrior,' he says.

Sabo interrupts. 'May I talk to you in the trailer?'

EIGHT

Jackson and I take a seat on the kick pads in the trailer. Sabomin stands in front of a pile of vertically stacked practice mats that looks like a giant wafer biscuit. When I woke up this morning, I didn't expect to be spending my afternoon in a sweltering trailer with martial arts experts. But nothing about today has been normal.

'You killed that board,' Sabomin says.

My heart beats near my tonsils. I can't speak.

'So,' Sabomin says, 'tell me if any of this sounds familiar. Dizziness, hot flushes, nausea, your hands and torso start flashing invisible and suddenly you can fight like Jackie Chan?'

The air sucks out of the trailer, my stomach squelches, my hands slide down to my knees with sweat. Nervousness creeps all over me as panic climbs in my chest. 'Um,' I stutter, my cheeks stinging with a vicious blush. Jackson will think I'm a freak, a total weirdo, if I admit to flashes of invisibility.

'You, my girl, have the symptoms of ninja,' Sabomin says.

Jackson slaps the back of his hand on his palm. 'Textbook,' he says. 'Let's take her down to the dojang and see what she can do!'

His excitement is almost more than I can take. Instead of wanting to hide, I feel like running. But I stay where I am, for fear of leaving a sweat patch on the kick pad I'm sitting on.

Sabomin points the tip of his belt out the door of the trailer. 'To the dojang!' he cries theatrically.

Squeezed next to Jackson in the front of the van, I relish every bump in the road that pushes our knees together. My senses are brimming with his scent. I know I shouldn't be in a van with a stranger — Mum would kill me. But Jackson makes me feel safe. Protected.

Sabo pulls up in the forecourt of a service station. 'We're here,' he says.

'To fill up?' I ask.

'No.' Jackson leans over me to open the door and his hair brushes against my cheek. 'To fight.'

Nerves seize my stomach. I've already fought once today, but that was a total fluke. I couldn't possibly do it again. I don't know how.

The service station is ancient: petrol pumps without hose nozzles; an out-of-service car wash; an empty shop; graffitied concrete walls. I follow Sabo and Jackson around the back and down a driveway that leads to a blue building with a single black door and a red sticker saying *Get your kicks here.*

'You're going to love this,' Jackson says as he pulls the door open for me.

I'm not so sure.

I gasp as I enter the room. The floor is carpeted with spongy blue and red jigsaw mats. The walls are lined with sheets of white rice paper and etched with dark wooden beams that weave in intricate patterns up to the ceiling and spiral into a glass dome that infuses the room with a warm glow. The room contains every type of equipment you can imagine: kick bags hanging from the roof on chains, ladders, cones, bamboo sticks, swords, nunchucks and things I don't recognise. I am in awe of this room. There is a peacefulness to it that makes you feel instantly serene.

Jackson and Sabo bow as they enter.

'Welcome to the dojang,' Sabomin says. 'Operation ninjathon by day, kids' classes by night. Jacko here,' he slaps Jackson on the back, 'is one of my instructors.'

Sabo and Jackson disappear into a side room. I walk along the wall of the dojang and look at some of the equipment. One wall is adorned with hundreds of silver rings that seem to have claws attached to them. I pick one off the wall and fit it to my middle finger. When I close my fist, the claw pops out.

'Cool,' I gasp.

'Super cool,' Sabomin says.

I spin around, flustered, to see him wearing a fresh white Taekwondo uniform. Jackson is wearing a uniform too, but his is all black. He has a black hood wrapped around his head, leaving only his moss-green eyes visible.

He performs an axe kick followed by a 540-degree spinning roundhouse kick, double side kick into a double knife hand, finishing with percussive strikes. His stances zip, and as he spins on his heels his uniform cracks as if the sleeves have been dipped in starch and he has a cat-o'-nine-tails attached to each wrist. I'm still watching his hair fly and the black belt flick as he says, 'Cool, huh?'

Still in a daze, I don't respond.

'Rox?' he says.

I snap out of it. 'Awesome,' I say.

'This is the *shinobi shozoku*, secret uniform of the ninja,' he says, running his hands down his chest. 'This is a new model — there are compartments built into it for storing waste, so you can go without leaving any evidence when you're in enemy territory.'

'Like a wetsuit for surfers?' I say.

He laughs. 'Exactly.'

He begins explaining the parts of the uniform: the black jacket with its close-fitting sleeves and no cuffs or ties that could snag on any surfaces; the black pants that tuck into cloth gaiters wound around his calves; the soleless two-toed ninja slippers called *tabi*. 'The cloth of the trousers can be used for heaps of stuff,' he says. 'As a flotation device, or a tent or hammock. They're also reversible for camouflage — the reverse side is green for bush.'

'I get it,' I interrupt, becoming impatient. I don't care about his ninja pants and what they can do, I want to know why Hero hates me. 'Why am I here?'

But Jackson's so in love with his ninja suit he continues. 'The hood, or *zukin*, has been soaked in an antiseptic resin to be used as a bandage, or a filter to purify water for drinking. Cool, huh?'

Maybe the hood also makes you deaf.

'Jackson,' I try again. 'Why am I here?'

He looks at me with those leafy-green eyes. 'Okay, Roxy,' he holds out his hand, 'are you ready?'

I take his hand, feeling the pulsating warmth as I brush past his wrist. 'For what?'

He twists my wrist and I fly into the air, spin three times and land on my knees before him.

'To show us what you can do,' Sabo says. 'Jacko here has been ninjaing all on his own. Old man here,' Sabo rubs his heart again, 'is just a retired champion. Won myself a gold in the State championships of '73.' He takes a long, dragging breath and shakes his head. 'But now isn't the time to go on about the glory days. I know a special student when I train one, and Jackson, like you, was born special.'

I feel myself blush so hard the warmth of my cheeks practically steams up into my eyes. No one's ever called me special. Well, Elecktra has, but I don't think it was meant as a compliment. And not only does Sabo think I'm special, he's put me in the same category as Jackson — two special peas in a pod. Could this day get any weirder?

Jackson takes a bamboo stick off the wall and begins to twirl it around his body at lightning speed. The bamboo whirs in front of his face, fanning his blond hair off his forehead. Sabo nods to the wall and I pick out my own bamboo stick. It feels warm, seared by the many hands that have fought with it. At first, the stick feels clumsy in my hands and my wrists are stiff, but after a while I find I can spin the stick around my body, copying Jackson. We stand mirroring each other's movements. Jackson speeds up to challenge me. I'm up for it.

'Why do you need me?' I ask, spinning the stick.

Sabo moves between us like a referee and we stop spinning the sticks when we see the black velvet case in his hands. My questions vanish as he opens the case to reveal a set of glittering silver stars.

'*Shuriken*,' says Jackson, 'or throwing blades — a ninja's number one weapon, used to paralyse an opponent from afar.'

'The ninja star will show you who you are,' Sabo says.

I look down at the constellation of stars: they are all different, some with serrated edges, others with fat spikes, some with knife points, others with blunt points intended to maim rather than kill. I select a silver star with a serrated edge and an orchid symbol in the centre.

I hold the star in my hands and close my eyes.

A flash of shoulders, a scream, my mother's ponytail in my face — she's running, with me on her back. I'm a baby, no more than a year old. I clutch her neck for dear life. I feel something at my feet. I look down and see the head of a sword tucked into her black belt. There are men on horses charging after us, men in front of us. My mother is kicking and striking her way through the men, using her *katana* sword. Her sapphire-midnight hair gallops against her back as she spins. Her ninja *shinobi shozoku* and her porcelain cheeks are striped with warrior blood. She is panting white-hot breath into the night, her silver sword flashing light into her dark eyes.

A man with a sword approaches, his eyes red with rage. He lifts his sword. Mum reaches her elbow back behind her ear, lifting the ninja star past my cheek. The star has serrated edges and in its heart is an orchid. Just like the ninja star I now hold in my hands.

'Wow,' I whisper, opening my eyes. 'Mum's ninja star.'

I think back to the words my mother wrote yesterday on my hard-boiled egg: *Reach for the stars*. Maybe she meant ninja stars.

Sabo nods. 'Ninja is passed on strongest through the female line,' he says.

I've often wondered if there is any ninja in Elecktra or me. But Mum has always told me it's impossible because of who our father was. And our father remains a mystery.

I look at Jackson. He's smiling at me. 'And the White Warrior?' I ask.

'Legend has it, the White Warrior is born with the power to control the martial arts elements of wind, water, earth, fire and invisibility,' he says. 'He wears a white *shinobi shozoku* because of his amazing powers. Only one White Warrior is born every century — and they're hunted by the samurai and ninja clans, because if you kill a White Warrior you get his powers.' Jackson's eyes are intense.

'You want to kill the White Warrior?' I ask.

'No,' Sabo says, 'I want him for the demo team. Earthquakes, storms and all that — it'll be awesome!'

'You're not serious?' I say.

Jackson laughs. 'Long ago, the ninjas swore to protect the White Warrior, and in return the White Warrior protects the ninjas.'

'Against who?' I ask.

'The samurai, who still hunt the White Warrior. They want that power for themselves. As the Tiger Scrolls are the link to the White Warrior, Hero wants to find them first. If he succeeds, the ninja clan will lose all our protection and the samurai will become all-powerful.'

My heart traps in my throat. My saliva turns to cement. 'This must mean Hero is a samurai!' I blurt. This takes his bullying to a whole new level. *Hero is not just a bully; he's my mortal enemy,* I think as Jackson nods.

'How do I fit into all this?' I stammer.

'There're twice as many samurai as ninjas. Your ninjaism is just coming in and we need you on our side.'

I realise why Mum would never have mentioned the White Warrior. She didn't want me to be involved in this fight. She's always wanted me to be a normal kid. Not a ninja.

Jackson takes a star and throws it towards the ceiling. It flies up, past the beams, until it spears into the middle rafter, piercing it dead centre. Jackson turns and winks at me, causing my stomach to flutter. He is awesome at both art and ninja arts — what a legend.

Now it's my turn. I spin once, then let my star fly out of my hand. It circles us twice and returns to my hand. I try to throw it at the nearest wall, but again it circles us and returns to my hand. On my third try, the star slices through a punching bag, spraying sand across the mats, before rebounding to my hand.

'You've got a boomerang one!' Jackson says and slaps me hard on the back. I cough. 'We're really going to have some fun. Now put your hands like this, in the sign of water,' he says.

I place the star on the floor and copy the movement, making a fist with my right hand and pointing my left palm flat towards it, fingertips to my chin in a prayer position. My hands touch.

'No,' he says. 'Like this.' He makes the symbol again and this time I understand the microscopic distance between the two hands and copy him.

'If you can harness the power of rock,' he nods at his closed fist, 'and water,' he nods towards his open palm, 'and control both as separate entities within you, where nothing else exists, then you'll be able to control your invisibility.'

'Powerful stuff,' Sabo says. 'Classic ninja material.'

'I still don't understand why you need me,' I say, picking my star up again carefully, scared that it might do to me what it just did to the punching bag.

'Do you know the meaning of ninja?' Jackson asks.

I shake my head.

'Stealth. We're known as the shadow warriors.'

Stealth. There's nothing stealthy about Jackson. He's only been at the school a few days and every girl knows his name. He can't go anywhere without being noticed.

'The samurai were the rich warrior caste, and the ninja clan developed as a reaction against them,' he continues. 'They came from the poor farming communities who were barely surviving under samurai rule. They started out as thieves and then became the best spies in Japan — achieving missions by any means. For thousands of years, the ninjas and the samurai have been enemies. We use stealth. They use swords.'

I imagine Hero with a sword and my blood runs cold. Truly my mortal enemy.

'Eighty-seven years ago the ninja and samurai clans declared peace,' he says. 'Then a new White Warrior was born. The ninja clan kept their promise to protect the White Warrior, but the samurai still wanted to kill him to take his power. In order to protect her child from the samurai, the White Warrior's mother had his powers extracted by a mystic monk and placed into some scrolls. The Tiger Scrolls.'

'Wow,' I say.

Jackson narrows his brows and stares deep into my eyes. *This must be serious*, I tell myself.

'We need to find the current White Warrior and the Tiger Scrolls before Hero does, to prevent him and the samurai from taking the White Warrior's powers. We're talking clan war here, Roxy. If Hero succeeds, everyone we love will die.'

My heart throbs. Jackson's words echo into its chambers, where my mother and Art live, and Elecktra. Cinnamon too.

'Where do we start looking?' I ask.

'In the Cemetery of Warriors.'

'But where's that?'

'It's not of this world. You get transported there when the ancient warriors decide you're ready.'

'Transported to another world?' I can't believe what I'm hearing. I had no idea all this was going on around me. I have a different opinion of boring Lanternwood now — it's getting more exciting by the minute.

'The White Warrior bears a mark on his soul,' Jackson goes on. 'That's how we'll know it's the right person.'

How can you see a soul, let alone see a soul that's got a mark on it? Do you look down someone's throat to see a marked soul, or into their eyes? Or do you wait for them to cough? And why do Jackson and Sabo think I'll be able to help them? I can't even get through the school gates without being spat on. I have a hard enough time at school as it is, being harassed by Hero and his friends. Do I really need to take on all this ninja stuff as well?

'If I do help you find this White Warrior person and get back the scrolls, what's in it for me?' I ask.

'If you join us in this search, I'll give you something you really want,' Jackson says confidently.

I try to think of something I really want, but nothing matches up to the danger Jackson is proposing. Not even the thought of again being alone with him in the gym. I can't think of anything Jackson could give me to make me want to train night and day to track down some warrior. Then my palms become slippery and my crawling stomach tells me there is something I want more than anything, but I lack the guts to say it.

Jackson says it for me. 'I'll make you Gate One.'

NINE

A crowd of five-year-olds bursts through the dojang doors. Two mothers carrying large birthday cakes and balloons call out to Sabo: 'Where should we put the fairy bread?'

'The trestle table.' Sabo points to the table at the front of the dojang.

'Sorry,' Jackson says to me. 'Forgot we had a birthday party today.'

'Good extra business. Hour or so of ninja games, half-hour to eat,' Sabo adds. 'We have a few each week.'

'Beats a clown,' I say.

The mothers put out party hats, plates of fairy bread, party pies and red cordial. I can't believe they've actually brought red cordial and remember how banned it is at home.

The kids are swarming around the dojang. Jackson calls them over to a mat. They run over and sit down.

'Who wants to be a ninja?' he yells.

The children cheer excitedly.

'But before we can *be* ninjas, we've gotta *look* like ninjas,' he says.

Sabo wheels over a rack of multicoloured Taekwondo suits, and he and Jackson commence the job of dressing a large group of wriggly children and tying white belts around their waists. I help.

'What's your name?' I ask a little boy.

'Charles,' he says.

'How old are you?'

'Free.'

I smile as I tie the belt around his tiny body and he shoots off to play with the other children.

Once the kids are dressed, Sabo organises them into two lines. He and Jackson punch a small soft yellow ball with a smiley face to the first child in each line, who has to kick it, run to retrieve it and deliver it back to the instructor.

'My feet are glued to this kick pad,' Jackson tells one kid who refuses to fetch the ball. 'If I step off it, I'll get eaten by the sharks.' He points to the blue mats surrounding them.

The child races after the ball.

Sabo throws me his ball and steps off his kick pad. 'Sharks, sharks!' the children scream. Sabo goes over to talk to the mums and has them giggling within seconds as he helps to cover more buttered bread with coloured sprinkles. I take his spot on the kick pad and begin throwing the ball to the children. Jackson smiles at me and nods approvingly, the gold speckles in his eyes flashing.

There are almost thirty children and their screaming and laughing are deafening. Jackson stops the game and calls the children in. 'Now for a bit of ninja stealth,' he says and smiles.

The children jitter around our waists.

'This is Foxy Roxy,' he says, indicating me, 'and you're all rabbits. If a fox catches you,' he continues, twisting his black belt around so the ends stick out at the back like a tail, 'you have to sit quietly in the fox's den off to the side.'

The kids scream and disperse, fizzing from one end of the room to the other. Jackson and I are super quick, darting between them, trying to give the slower ones more time to play. Within minutes we have caught all the rabbits.

'Again!' Jackson calls.

The kids jump up from the den and scatter, screaming.

'Out of curiosity,' I say, 'what happens when someone reaches the other world?'

'They have to defeat four ancient warriors in the Cemetery of Warriors,' he says.

'Dead guys?'

'Dead masters of martial arts,' he corrects me. 'If all four ancient warriors are defeated, the White Warrior will appear.'

'Is that it?' I say, knowing it is more than enough.

'Cake time,' Sabo calls.

Lighting the birthday candles is hard work. One child keeps spitting on them to blow them out and the birthday kid starts crying. By the time we finally make it to 'Happy Birthday', the kids are bored. It's up to Jackson and me to sing. I'm embarrassed to sing in front of him, but he starts off with such gusto I feel bad and join in.

When the song finishes, Jackson leans in close and says, 'You've got courage.' I feel goose bumps on my neck. 'And all-right reflexes,' he adds. His breath tickles my ear. 'I can train you to help me find the White Warrior and the Tiger Scrolls.'

He pulls away and my neck stings cold again.

'Hip hip!' he yells.

The children yell back: 'Hooray!'

The party finishes and the kids clear out. We are left with spilled cordial, cake crumbs smudged on the floor, scattered coloured sprinkles, and miniature uniforms and belts strewn all over the mats. Jackson begins to clean up.

'And the Cemetery of Warriors doesn't exist in this realm?' I say.

'Nope.'

'How many realms are there?'

'Not exactly sure.'

'Why don't you do it yourself?' I ask.

'He can't,' Sabo says, overhearing. 'He's already been transported once.'

I stare at Jackson. 'You've been to the Cemetery of Warriors?!'

He doesn't answer me.

'He defeated one warrior, but that's it,' Sabo says.

'She doesn't need to know that,' Jackson says and storms off.

'It's a bit of a sensitive subject,' Sabo whispers, so Jackson doesn't hear.

Jackson returns with a mop and takes out his anger on the mats until they shine like mirrors. When the dojang is spotless again, he approaches me with a black square of folded fabric.

'Ready to suit up?' he asks.

I push the uniform away. 'I'm sorry,' I tell him. 'This isn't me.'

'What do you mean? The *shinobi shozoku* is flattering on any type of body,' Sabo says. He rubs his big belly. 'It covers a lot.'

'I don't mean the uniform,' I say. 'I'm sorry. I've already done things today I would never ordinarily do.'

Jackson studies my face. 'Maybe that's a good thing,' he says.

'I have to go,' I say. 'Thank you for the ...' I hesitate, searching for a word to summarise my first dojang experience, 'information.'

When I reach the door, I turn to see Sabo and Jackson still standing where I left them. I bow at the dojang entrance, as I saw them do earlier. When I slide my fists down my thighs, I suddenly realise my hands are invisible again. Panic pounces. I'm going to have to find some other way to deal with what's happening to me, which doesn't involve getting killed.

TEN

As soon as I walk into our living room, Elecktra yells, 'Sending that photo was totally unfair! You have to make it up to me! You owe me a makeover!'

She's wearing a pink jumpsuit with yellow wedge sandals and her forearms are stacked with bangles. Her eyes are still the colour of warm bark despite her mood. She's spread out her make-up on the green rug and the coloured palettes look like bright flowers growing out of a lawn. Elecktra often plays with her make-up when she should be studying. Art says it's the artist in her, but I don't think our school careers counsellor was thinking make-up artist when Elecktra said she wanted to follow in Mum's boyfriend's footsteps.

'You made me strip off in front of your friends!' I yell back.

'You were ruining my T-shirt!' she squarks.

'Girls,' Art calls from the kitchen, where he and his friend Hacky are talking about Art's next exhibition and drinking tea. Art knows better than to interfere in our fights.

'You know I love that T-shirt!' Elecktra throws an eyeliner at me. 'Do you want me to tell that new boy you think he's cute?'

'I do not!' I spear the eyeliner back at Elecktra. It hits her in the chest and she immediately checks to see if it has left a mark on her bright pink jumpsuit. Luckily for me, it hadn't.

'You do so! I saw you staring at him!' she squeals, then sings, 'Roxy loves the new boy.'

'Do not!'

'You could be his It Girl!'

'I don't want to be his It Girl,' I retort.

'Come on — you owe me,' she whines. 'Makeover!'

'Elecktra, no. Anything but a makeover,' I plead.

The last makeover Elecktra gave me, she waxed my top lip and I had to wear a Band-Aid over it until it healed. The kids at school teased me and said that I was trying to hide a moustache.

I know Elecktra won't give up. 'Stubborn' is her middle name.

She looks up from the soft-pink blush palette she's holding.

'I'm designing,' she says.

'Designing what?' Art asks, having come to see what all the noise and fuss were about.

'Fash …' she pauses for effect, 'ion. FashION for the face,' she adds, heading for her room.

Art looks confused, but I understand her 'Elecktrafied' language, and I need to talk to her. I need answers, even if I have to go through a makeover to get them. Finally, I build up the courage and knock on her white bedroom door without its porcelain doorknob.

'Go away, I'm rehearsing!' she yells.

'For what?' I call back.

'Actressing.'

I unscrew the white porcelain doorknob from my bedroom door and fit it into the gaping hole in Elecktra's door, then gently turn it. Her door clicks open.

'What did you do?' she screams.

'You can keep carrying your doorknob around in your school bag if you like,' I say, 'but all doorknobs fit all doors in this house, so it won't keep anyone out.'

She flies towards me, enraged. She's changed into a long multicoloured kaftan that makes her movements more dramatic — she looks like a human kaleidoscope. As she tries to slam the door in my face, I'm struck by whatever sickening sweet perfume she's lathered on her neck. It smells like crayons on a melting car dashboard and nearly causes me to give up.

'I can't wait to tell Mum and Art about you wagging school,' she says, pushing with all her strength on the door, squeezing my shoulders against the doorframe. She isn't as strong as me. I punch the door.

'What the —?!' Elecktra screams.

I look at the door and realise I have punched a dent in it. I'm not used to my new strength. I am so in trouble. First, I ruined her top, then wagged school, and now I've vandalised her door.

'I'm telling!' she yells.

I grab her arm firmly and squeeze my voice soft. 'Please, Lecky, please don't,' I beg.

Elecktra huffs and shakes her arm free of my grip with a symphony of bangles on her wrist. She abandons the futile pushing and suddenly asks, 'You know that new kid?'

I stop breathing.

'I think I should be *his* It Girl,' she says.

I look away to hide my dread. I want to keep Jackson Axe mine, my friend.

Elecktra combs her fingers through her wispy fringe. 'He's in my year,' she says, looking at me from under the branches of her thick eyelashes. 'Why's he friends with *you*?'

I'm frozen. The word 'friend' floats down onto my heart. He is *my* friend.

Lecky rests her chin to the side and sighs, flipping her voice over her shoulder. 'Anyways, it doesn't count that he's in my *year*, he just better be in my *league*,' she says. 'Contestant on any reality TV shows?'

'Don't think so,' I manage to stutter.

She saunters back to the mirror and pouts at her reflection. I can't swallow the threat of losing Jackson to Elecktra.

'I thought you were going to tell the careers counsellor you wanted to be a celebrity stylist,' I say. 'What happened to forecasting *pirate chic*?' Elecktra twirls on the spot, instantly refocused on herself. The best thing about Elecktra is that you can manipulate her mood swings.

'Nope. I wanted to be a stylist, then a social media guru, but why be a stylist when you can be an actress and be *on* the red carpet.'

She performs an animated silent mime in the mirror. I think she's pretending to interview herself, but I can't quite tell. I sit down on her bed. Her room is a mix of childhood and older girl. A ladybug lamp sits on a nest of *Vogue* magazines and there are high heels and stuffed animals all over the floor.

'Lecky, can I ask you a question?' I say.

'You just have,' she says.

She turns towards me, but as she casts a look back over her shoulder at her reflection, I realise it's only so she can admire her beauty from another angle.

'Have you ever been invisible?' I continue, hoping to raise a morsel of interest. Trying to have a conversation with my sister is hard work.

'What, like a ghost?' she says, whipping her head around to me. She picks up a hair roller and puts it into her fringe, pressing on it with all the force of someone thinking really, *really* hard, then releases the curl. She looks back in the mirror. 'Not bad,' she says admiringly. 'Don't believe in stupid ghosts,' she adds.

I sigh. Sometimes there's no point trying to talk to Elecktra about anything but herself. 'Good,' I say. 'When you die, you'll be too embarrassed to haunt me.'

'Why are you so weird?' she says. 'It's stuff like that'll make you Gate Two forever.'

Her words sting, striking me in the thatched part of my heart where all the taunts and teases entwine. I hate it when she's mean; it's the only thing that doesn't look good on her. I cross my legs and drop my head to my lap.

'You really should get that lasered off, or fake-tan it.' Elecktra's pointing at the birthmark on the bottom of my foot.

She's always going on about my birthmark. I rub my feet on her bedspread and she shrieks and jumps on me.

We wrestle until we exhaust ourselves. I untangle myself from her kaftan, roll away from her and try again.

'Lecky, don't you ever wake up and feel like you're different?'

'Nope,' she says. 'Sometimes I wake up with a serious case of bad hair day, but that's it.' She shrugs.

'Well, sometimes I feel like I'm adopted,' I say. 'Haven't you ever wondered why Mum won't tell us anything about Dad?'

Elecktra's not listening. 'Time to leave,' she says, shooing me away. 'I'm in the middle of a scene. Make sure you introduce me to that boy. Things didn't work out with Jarrod.'

She slams the door and the lockout explodes the loneliness within me. I take back my door handle and slink to my room.

That night I stand at my window, watching the shadows play across the pavement. The street is lined with houses, wheelie bins, gardens — and now ninjas and samurai. What do I care if Hero finds the White Warrior first? What real damage could he do? But I know the answer. Lots.

I look over at my school bag on the floor. Jackson must have stuffed the *shinobi shozoku* in there and now it's calling to me.

'Be quiet,' I tell it.

I maroon myself in the island of light created by my desk lamp and fold paperclips into tiny coathangers to take my mind off it. But the uniform starts calling: *Come on! Try me on! It won't hurt! No one will know!*

I pick up a book and try to read, but the only words filling my mind are: *Try me on now.*

'Okay!' I say.

I rush over to the bag and shake out the uniform. I wrap the jacket over my black T-shirt, tie my hair in a bun and fold the hood over my head, secure the pants into the cloth boots and strap them up. I finish by tying a belt around my waist. I turn slowly to see my reflection in the window. I look strong and confident. My eyes are wild. Forget pirate chic, this is the first time I have ever looked daring, the first time I've ever looked like ... me, Roxy Ran.

My eyes pierce my reflection ... but I am not alone. Over my shoulder, another set of eyes glitters in the glass. Before I can react, the window is opened and I fling myself through it and onto the ledge of the roof.

I run, jumping across gutters, driveways, rubbish bins, dog kennels. I look back and see a dark figure chasing me, silhouetted against the light of the moon. My eyes water from my speed and I find it easy to grip in the boots and leap higher than I could ever imagine.

I can fly over houses, land on the footpath and then leap to the top of a tree, tiptoe across power lines. My pursuer can also leap and fly. I glance behind me again and a blinding flash awakens my fear. A sword. I have no weapons, only the camouflage of my black uniform in the night. There is no time to will myself invisible — even if I knew how.

I feel my pursuer gaining on me. Suddenly, feet land in front of me and I look up to see dangerous eyes staring at me. A sword is at my throat. In this moment, on top of a terracotta-tiled roof, I realise my life has changed forever.

'Mum!' I gasp. 'It's me!'

Mum's eyes are coal-coloured, hypnotic.

'Mum, put down the *katana* sword — it's me.' I swipe the hood off my head. 'Roxy.'

Mum's eyes widen and envelop the night. She is in her gym gear: black tights and black lycra hooded top. Her hair has fallen out in the chase and is flickering wildly around her. She has never looked more lovely. She pulls back the sword.

'What are you wearing?' she pants. 'I thought you were an intruder!'

I shrug. 'Ninja suit.'

'It's called a *shinobi shozoku*,' she says crisply, yanking my wrist so I stoop down. She scuttles on all fours to the top of the roof and down the other side, pulling me with her. Now we can't be seen from the street.

'I've been picked to help find the White Warrior,' I say proudly, standing up. She yanks me back down.

The night fills her eyes. 'What?'

'The White Warrior. You should know,' I say. 'The warrior born every century with the power to control the elements. But the powers were taken from him and put in a book or something.'

Mum screws her mouth tight. I see a storm building within her. 'The Tiger Scrolls,' she whispers, darting her eyes around us.

'I met this boy at school, Jackson, and we're going to find the White Warrior before Hero does.'

I can't believe how excited I feel telling her this. For the first time in my life, I belong to something, and it's not just a book club or choir, or a group of fakeys like Elecktra's friends, but a ninja clan.

'You should have told me the legend,' I say. 'And what's going on with Hero. No wonder he hates me. He's samurai!'

'Shhhhhh,' Mum whispers. A cloud moves over the moon, ushering a foreign darkness across her cheeks. She looks transformed — young, threatening and ruthless, but still looking around feverishly. What is she so afraid of?

Mum reaches up and pulls my hood back over my head. She looks over her shoulder, then stands up. She gives me the look I grew up with: *Do not disobey me.* I'm longing to know where I came from, why I have these powers, but before I can say anything, Mum launches at me with the sword.

I leap backwards, just in time to avoid my stomach being slashed. 'Mum!' I scream. Tears spark in my eyes.

Mum is unperturbed and runs at me at full speed, as if the roof was made of slippery ice. I tell my body to be still and quiet, but the fire returns and there is no way to extinguish it. Mum bends her knees to jump and, as she takes off, I reach up and grab her ankles. With a flick of my wrist, she's spinning in the air. She releases the sword and I catch it, jump high, my knees lifting up to my ears, and land with my feet either side of her cheeks, yoking her neck to the ground, the point of the sword an eyelash from her retina.

We stare each other down until a sound in the bushes below distracts me. She flips me over by sweeping my heels, and before I can breathe, I feel the pressure of the sword pinning down my shoulder. Mum's blonde mane flickers around her shoulders like fire. My heart stops.

The sword is powerful, her most deadly weapon: a long blade with a red leather handle and Japanese writing at the tip. It is the sword I saw in my memory earlier today, when I was strapped to her back and she was fighting the samurai. I've never really asked her any questions before. Aside from the self-defence training she taught Elecktra and me, I know very little about martial arts. But now I want to know everything.

I don't dare swallow or take my eyes off her. Her bottom lip quivers, her breath smells of Hulk juice, words form on her tongue. I open my ears to hear her clearly. 'It's finally happening,' she says.

Then she kisses me on the head and says, 'I have to leave. Tell your sister to behave,' and backflips away onto a neighbour's roof.

I watch her soaring over the rooftops until she disappears, a shadow slipped into darkness.

ELEVEN

Saturday breakfast is usually wholewheat blueberry pancakes with beetroot and honey muffins. But today Art is making pancakes the ordinary way out of a shaker bottle and Elecktra is sponging them in maple syrup that she found in the bowels of our kitchen cupboards. Last night feels like a dream. I rub the small hole in my skin where the tip of Mum's sword nicked me. I can't have dreamed that. Her attack has turned my bones to foam. I feel like I'm drowning in disbelief.

'So Mum's gone?' I ask Art.

'She's away on business again. Won't be back for a while,' he says.

'How long?' I ask.

'Few weeks. She'll send us SMS updates as usual, but she said she'll be out of range for the most part.'

This is not unusual for Mum. She often disappears for weeks at a time. We have no real idea where she travels to, but it must be somewhere in Asia because last time she returned with a black eye and told us she'd fallen off a rickshaw.

'What does Mum do again anyway?' Elecktra asks, as she does whenever Mum goes away. She can never remember.

'Your mother is a very successful financial advisor,' Art says. 'You know that.'

'Oh, yeah,' Elecktra says, sucking maple syrup out of her nails. When she's done, she sprinkles icing sugar onto a bowl of cereal.

'We're not allowed cereal for breakfast. "Cereal killers" — full of sugar, remember?' I say, repeating what Mum tells us whenever we rebel against her zero-sugar warrior diet. It's beginning to make more sense to me now.

'Elecktra offered to make breakfast,' Art says, waving his spoon at me. 'A day off won't hurt.' He carries his own bowl of cereal and icing sugar to the table. Art had to give up sugar when he met my mother and he'll take any excuse to have a taste again.

'Relax, Rox,' Elecktra says.

'You relax,' I shoot back.

'Both of you relax,' Art says. 'Go put a yellow ribbon in your hair,' he tells me.

'Why?' My hand's shaking as I take celery out of the fridge to prepare the Hulk juice. Even though I don't really like Hulk juice, the ritual makes me miss Mum less. Now Mum's gone, what do I do about my ninjaism?

'Yellow to honour your solar plexus. To calm you down,' Art says.

If Mum's not going to give me answers, I'll have to ask the internet. I sit down with my laptop.

Mum doesn't talk much about her ninja days or where she was born. Sometimes I'll see her practising her stances on the clothesline in Ms Winters's backyard and she always makes the bed using ninja techniques: a knife-hand strike to fold the corners, outside block to hook the corners, then a spear-hand strike to smooth the sheet down, followed by a spinning hook kick to slam the pillows against the headboard. She once told me that it was hard to retire her ninja suit and she still craves it. Sometimes I'll catch her doing the housework with a T-shirt on her head, the arms tied around the back of her neck and only her eyes visible through the neck hole. I know she has to make a conscious effort to walk slowly in supermarkets, not climb the shelves or leap from aisle to aisle, and to be patient in traffic and not lose her temper. Mum can have lethal road rage.

As I trawl through the internet, I discover that, once upon a time, the ninja nemesis was the Giant White Tiger. I wonder if Mum ever fought a tiger. These ancient tigers could fly and also had powers of invisibility. The ninjas and the Giant White Tigers finally reconciled, so now the ninja enemy is the samurai. We are mortal enemies, which means we must kill each other no matter what. I click the mouse furiously as images of ninjas in their black uniforms and red samurai with their powerful swords invade the screen.

The ninja clan fights with stealth and skill, the samurai fight with sword. Samurai have always hated us for fighting in the shadows, but that's the only way we know how. I learn that we were poor farmers who couldn't afford metal for swords. Unlike the samurai, who came from the Japanese military class and wore clothes coloured with bright red expensive dyes. The samurai value honour over everything; they'll cut their own throats before dishonouring their clan. They live according to the Bushido code that means 'Way of the Warrior'. I search 'Bushido code' and realise it's a code of conduct similar to the European etiquette of a man opening a door for a lady — and still exists in dojos today.

Ninjas, on the other hand, weren't upper class. They won't open doors for you, but blow them up instead! They were from feudal Japan and nicknamed 'stealers'. Espionage and assassination were their speciality. Their stealth warfare led to stealth weapons such as nunchucks and ninja stars. They achieve a mission by whatever means necessary; sneak attacks, poison, seduction and spying are all fair game, but for the samurai, those tactics are loathed. Legend has it the best ninjas can turn invisible and fly.

My heart pounds. I've never seen Mum flash invisible. I've never even seen her fly before. I continue reading, my mind pummelled by information.

There are more samurai than ninjas because, in the 1600s, the samurai set out to annihilate all the ninjas. Ninja and samurai clans still exist today, fighting in secret, protecting their family honour and their clans, like the Mafia.

The war between ninja and samurai clans changed the role of the ninja — the samurai became the warrior cast and ninjas had to go underground. They went from warriors to secret police, but as the older generations of ninjas died, there were fewer young men prepared to do the hard training it takes to become a ninja. Poverty forced the boys to give up spying and training and go to work instead, leaving their wives at home. So it became the women's job to train their little ninjas. They would train several hours a day. Hence ninja was passed on mostly through the females.

My nose is almost touching the screen when I finally find the legend of the White Warrior, a special warrior who has the power to control the elements of martial arts: wind, water, earth, fire and invisibility. 'The White Warrior must consume the Tiger Scrolls to unleash their powers,' I read aloud. 'There is only one White Warrior born every century. He is the most venerated and hunted human on the planet.'

My eyes widen. No wonder Jackson wants to find the White Warrior! The ninjas haven't been safe for eighty-seven years.

I lean back in my chair to take in the information, and even with all this research, my mind swims to thoughts of Jackson. I've never been friends with a boy before and the excitement of this overpowers the fear of samurai finding the White Warrior first. I pick up the phone next to my bed and dial Cinnamon. She answers.

'It's Rox,' I say.

'Where have you been? I thought we were going to see Elf?' she mumbles. I can tell she has food in her mouth.

'I'm so sorry, I forgot! I got caught up.' I dig my nails into my legs.

'But you spit swore. I can't believe it, Roxy,' she says, still chewing.

'We can go next week. Promise.'

Cinnamon doesn't say anything, but she never stays mad for long. I desperately want to tell her that the reason I forgot to hang out was the war between ninjas and samurai over the hunt for the White Warrior, but I'm not sure she would believe me. So, knowing she'll be interested, I mention Jackson.

'I met a boy,' I say.

Cinnamon gasps. 'A boy?!'

'Yeah, a *really cute* boy,' I say. Telling Cinnamon feels like opening a present; I'm ecstatic with anticipation. This must be why Elecktra prefers to talk about boys all day with her friends than actually date them.

'What's his name?' Cinnamon asks.

'Jackson Axe. He has blond hair. He's in Elecktra's year,' I say.

Silence.

'You like an older guy?' Cinnamon says slowly.

My heart sinks. He would never think I'm hot like my sister. He thinks I'm adorkable. A boy in Year Ten would never go for a little Year Seven — especially a girl who gets *worst dressed* every casual clothes day and has visibility issues. At least I could get us into the movies two for the price of one.

'Can I meet him?' Cinnamon squeals.

'Soon,' I promise. 'But you'll have to play it cool.'

'Ice cold,' Cinnamon agrees.

Suddenly, my bedroom door explodes inwards; Elecktra's frame fills the doorway, a towel turbaned over her freshly washed hair.

'I'm going to the DVD store in ten minutes, wanna come?' she asks.

I'm amazed she is even asking me to go with her. 'Sure,' I say. 'Can I choose?'

'Depends.' She shrugs. 'If it's got vampires or pirates, then no. But if there's a wedding, or a proposal, or a makeover scene, then yes.' She smiles.

Lecky *can* be nice. If only she realised that you don't have to be mean to get attention. She can be silly, vain and ridiculous, but when no one else is around and it's just us, I feel like I'm the only person who really gets her. It's a love-hate thing. It's a sister thing.

At the DVD store Elecktra heads straight to the romantic comedies and selects an old classic, *Father of the Bride*. The movie was made before she was born, but Elecktra loves Steve Martin and the chaotic wedding preparations. She is obsessed with weddings and has already designed her own wedding dress. She has locked me in as a bridesmaid on one condition: I wear a red dress. Of her choice.

I head over to the action movies section where I pick up a Jackie Chan film — the one with Jet Li. The cover shows Jet Li doing a kick through the air. I love this film.

Elecktra comes over and takes the DVD from me.

'You and Mum are just the same,' she says. 'Just because you look alike doesn't mean you can fight like her. She dyes her hair to be like me, remember?'

'No, she doesn't,' I say.

Elecktra sighs. I know she hates looking different from Mum and me.

'Don't you want to watch something romantic, with no fighting?' She holds up my Jackie Chan movie in one hand and her chick flick in the other. I look at the two films in her hands; they couldn't be more opposite, just like me and Elecktra. She likes chick flicks, I like action. She is blonde, my hair is black. She is tall, I am short. Her bedroom is a bomb site, I'm a neat freak. She is popular, I'm not. Could we be more different? We have the same mother, but sometimes Elecktra acts like she's come from outer space. She can be so alien to me. Elecktra rattles her film, trying to persuade me.

'Come on, Cat, the father is so nice in it,' she says. 'He just wants his daughter to have the most beautiful wedding ever.' Her eyes dim a little. Sometimes I see a hint of sadness simmering under the surface of her confident exterior, as though she wears a mask.

'How many times have you seen it?' I ask.

'Not enough. Oh, come on,' she pleads.

I think Lecky loves the film because despite all her wedding plans she still doesn't know who will walk her down the aisle. I think we have both always hoped our real father would be at our weddings.

'I guess we could watch both,' I say.

Elecktra narrows her eyes. 'Okay,' she agrees, 'but you have to let me buy us some chocolate as a treat and not tell Mum.'

She gives me a little grin as she puts out her pinkie finger and we pinkie swear like we used to when we were little.

Walking home with Elecktra, she asks me if I thought the new guy working at the DVD store was cute, and as usual I have to say I didn't notice ... because it is true. She teases me and calls me hopeless and we laugh and talk like sisters should.

And for a moment, I feel as though I could tell Elecktra about what I'm going through. Maybe she has experienced ninja too and didn't tell me about it.

I'm deep in thought when we arrive home. I see the note on the front door before Elecktra even notices it. It has my name on it. I rip it open, but as soon as I read it I feel my heart clunk and I'm thrown straight from a rom-com into a horror film.

I know what you are. You will never be safe again — I'll make sure of it. And if I find out you're even looking for the White Warrior, I'll hurt you. H.

My body writhes with fear at the thought of seeing Hero at school on Monday. There's no escaping this now. Clearly I am turning ninja and can't turn back. The only person who can help me is Jackson.

TWELVE

Elecktra slams the front door, then waits at the gate for me. She's wearing red boy's boxer shorts underneath her school skirt, and after waiting thirty seconds, she walks off. Today I won't be walking to school with Lecky. I've found a better way.

I stuff my ninja uniform into my backpack and open my bedroom window. I pull the ninja hood over my head. It totally complements my school uniform. Elecktra would call it 'ninja chic'. I take a deep breath and launch myself out of the window onto the roof. Leap over Ms Winters's house, then the next house and the next. I jump over gardens, kick over trellises, flip over fences. I feel light, agile, fast and furious. Going to school 'the top way' totally beats taking the 'bottom way' — down there with Elecktra, where insults seem to pile up like hard rubbish on the nature strips and in the gutters. I'm going to fly to school every day from now on. Flying at this speed, the wind stings my eyes.

I'm so high I can smell the rain in the clouds. Up here, all my problems seem to shrink. I refuse to be invisible. I refuse to live one more day being bullied by Hero and his clan.

I leap off the last house and land on the footpath three blocks from school. I remove my ninja hood and pack it into my school bag. I see Elecktra sauntering ahead and walk the rest of the way behind her.

I walk to Gate Two to wait for Jackson. No one makes Gate One first week of school — except Elecktra, that is. He's already there, on the footpath. He looks so handsome in his school uniform and I'm not the only one to have noticed. Girls are swarming around him, trying to get his attention. Even those who seem not to notice him are only doing it for effect.

I cup my hands to my mouth and call, 'Jackson!'

When he looks up, those fiery eyes hit me in the gut.

'Heyeee!' Elecktra screams. 'I know you!' She swaggers towards him. 'I know a friend of yours,' she says.

As I stand with the Gate Two wimps, geeks and misfits, all nervously building their courage before they run the gauntlet of Hero's spit brigade, I see Elecktra touch Jackson's arm. Seeing him with her tightens the fabric of my heart; a stitch pulls.

'Jackson!' I yell again.

When he links arms with Elecktra and steps through Gate One, the fabric tears into a gaping hole.

I'll give you something you really want, I remember Jackson saying. Well, he has just proved he can deliver.

Cinnamon runs over. 'Where is he?' she pants excitedly. I hardly notice her. I can't take my eyes off Elecktra and Jackson. Cinnamon follows my gaze.

'That him with Elecktra?' she asks thinly.

I nod, damming the tears by refusing to blink.

'Sorry, Rox,' she says, rubbing my back. 'Lecky seems to get them all.'

Not this one, I think. I swallow hard, blink, a tear glistens on my cheek.

The boy I like could end up with my sister and Hero's message is still firing at the front of my mind. He's going to make life hell today and if I knew how to be a ninja I could cope with it, but I don't. I'm a pathetic Gate Twoer who can't even tell a guy she *likes* him.

When I turn to Cinnamon, I see her hair is as wild as ever; thick curls sail in the wind. Parts of her face are painted monster green.

'Cim,' I begin to ask, but when her eyes set sadly on Hero and his friends loitering inside Gate Two, I stop. Now is not the time.

Bruce snarls at me; he has a strapped hand from our fight last week. Hero has a black eye that looks like hundreds of purple spiders have crawled under his skin and exploded. No one has ever stood up to him before, and he won't want anyone to know it was a Year Seven who gave him a dose of his own poison.

Cinnamon is shaking, setting her red afro abuzz. The bullies have already started yelling at her.

'Long sleeves today!' Hero shouts. 'Hiding your porky arms?'

Cinnamon pulls her sleeves down over her wrists and closes her eyes. We have a short-sleeved and long-sleeved school shirt option. I know Cinnamon usually wears the long sleeves because the short sleeves dig into her arms. I hear her whisper 'Rescue' under her breath. Our school counsellor has advised the Gate Twoers to find ourselves a 'happy word' to help us deal with bullies. A happy word isn't going to stop Hero and his clan spitting on us. Despite the constant anti-bullying workshops the school has us involved in, the bully-blocking program is clearly not working. School counsellors should spend less time in their offices and more time in the playground.

'Did you get an invite to Chantell's?' Cinnamon asks, opening her eyes and turning to where Chantell is handing out clutch-sized pink envelopes.

'Nup.' I try to sound unperturbed. It doesn't work. I stutter on the P. 'You?' I ask.

Cinnamon rattles her afro.

'Why don't we go anyway?' I suggest.

Cinnamon shakes her chin vehemently as Rescue pops his tiny head out of her pocket. I'm surprised she's brought him to school again, but she tells me she'll be leaving him in her locker. I guess he'll just spend the day sleeping. It'll certainly be safer there than in the toilets.

Inside Gate One, I see Jackson with Elecktra. They're facing one another and talking; it looks like she's interviewing him to see if he's a suitable date for the red carpet that exists in her mind.

'C'mon,' I tell Cinnamon, pulling her away from the gate.

'Where are we going?' she asks.

'To class,' I say, taking her hand.

'But class is through Gate Two,' Cinnamon objects.

'No. We're taking Gate Three today.'

'What do you mean Gate Three?'

'The top way,' I say. 'Assembly doesn't start for another twenty minutes, so we have time.'

I walk well away from the school gates and she follows me reluctantly. 'We could get into trouble. Someone will see us,' she says, grimacing.

'No one ever looks up,' I tell her.

Cinnamon keeps checking over her shoulder for teachers. Her afro tickles my ear every time she turns her head.

'Okay. We're here,' I say.

Cinnamon looks around, confused. 'Where's Gate Three?'

'Up there.' I point to the nearest roof.

I drop my bag and take out my ninja hood. I put it on.

Cinnamon laughs. 'What are you doing?' Her face is still the colour of Shrek, but I can't ask her why until Hero's taunts have worn off.

'I'm going to tell you a big secret,' I say. 'But you must promise not to tell ANYBODY.' Cinnamon steps closer and leans in, crosses her heart with her finger. I see total honesty in the depths of her oceanic-blue eyes and my secret spills forth. I tell her about my ninja encounter with Jackson, the hunt for the White Warrior, our mission to defeat the ancient masters in the Cemetery of Warriors. Cinnamon is captivated by my every word. I exaggerate my story with an eyebrow symphony, arching them up, plunging them down, and my hood adds extra flair.

'Wow,' she says at the end of it. 'That's the coolest thing I've ever heard.'

I don't think anyone has ever said anything I told them was cool before. I grin.

'I promise I won't tell anyone you're turning ninja,' Cinnamon says. 'I thought I noticed your invisible hands, but didn't know if it was real or not. So, where's this Gate Three then?'

I take her hand again and turn us to face the brick terrace house beside us. I have no idea if this will work. I close my eyes as I did when I was holding the ninja star and a flash of my mother chasing me over the rooftops with crazed power and skill fills my mind. I open my eyes, feeling peaceful. In broad daylight we might be caught, but that makes it all the more exciting.

'On three,' I say, 'jump.'

Cinnamon nods, then says, 'Wait!' She lifts Rescue out of her pocket and tucks him into her school bag, then zips it up. 'As Sergeant Major would say, "Ready ready."' She mimics his gruff voice.

Cinnamon's courage today is impressive. I hope this works. I shake out my legs to limber up. Twist my arms around my torso, crack my neck, then take two deep breaths.

'Three!' I yell.

We both jump at the same time, and in a leap I fly Cinnamon up to the roof of the house.

'Oh my goodness!' Cinnamon screams, looking

down at the street. 'This is totally awesome!' She giggles with excitement. 'How'd you learn that?'

'Apparently, it's all there, in me. I just have to learn how to use it. Want to try again?'

'Ready ready!' she squeals excitedly.

I take her hand and fly her over a driveway. Her brilliant red hair crackles as we leap from rooftop to rooftop, giggling. I concentrate on powering us forwards with the fire in my blood; that same fire that burned in the playground and singed the bench. I feel the air pockets bursting on my face as we slice through the air, hand in hand. As we near the school, I veer us to the right and we leap across the roof of the school building behind Gates One and Two. We come to a stop on the roof of the music department.

'We made it,' I say.

Cinnamon is buzzing. 'That felt like fireworks,' she says. 'Best ride I've ever been on!'

I smile the biggest grin. That means a lot, as she's one of the few people I've ever met who's actually been to Disneyland.

We jump down to the ground and I rip off my hood just as the bell rings and the hallway floods with kids on their way to assembly.

'Thanks,' Cinnamon says, hugging me. 'I've never done anything like that.'

'You know how Lecky always tells us to "get over ourselves"?' I say.

Cinnamon looks at me and nods.

'Well, I reckon she's right. Sometimes we do hold ourselves back.'

'I'm sick of being sweet and shy,' Cinnamon admits. 'Sometimes I wish I could be strong.'

'You can. Look at what you just did!'

She looks back over her shoulder at all the rooftops we flew over.

'Cim,' I say gently, 'what have you put on your face?'

She looks away. 'Mum's make-up.' She hesitates, then says, 'To cover up my —'

She doesn't finish, but I know what she means.

I study her face. 'It's a bit green,' I say.

'I used a paintbrush from the geography classroom,' she says, casting her eyes downwards and twisting in her shoes.

'Maybe it had a bit —'

But Cinnamon cuts me off. 'I'd rather be green than have pimples,' she says.

I hug Cinnamon. She wipes her chin on my school shirt, leaving a pale green smear. We giggle as we walk off to assembly.

THIRTEEN

I enter the dojang, bow and kneel in the centre of the mats.

'The *shinobi shozoku* looks good on you,' Jackson says, kneeling in front of me, wearing his ninja suit too.

So, I have commenced my ninja training. Pretty hardcore for a girl who wasn't even adorkable a few days ago. I feel so cool now! Jackson and Sabo have outlined a detailed program that's meant to get me ready to enter the Cemetery of Warriors to find the White Warrior.

My program is based on fourteen core martial arts principles:

1. *Mixed martial arts*
2. *Unarmed, hand-to-hand combat*
3. *Ninja stars and nunchucks*
4. *Spear and sword*
5. *Climbing*
6. *Elemental power: fire, explosives and water*

7. *Tying and escaping rope*
8. *Concealment*
9. *Magic*
10. *Espionage*
11. *Disguise*
12. *Stealth strategies*
13. *Bully blocking*
14. *Character building and spiritual awakening*

And five white-belt ninja skills:

1. *REAX (reflexes and reactions)*
2. *Ninja nutrition*
3. *Survival skills*
4. *Self-defence*
5. *Psychological warfare*

I know: piece of cake. If you're a baker. I've been a nobody my whole life and now I'm expected to be the best somebody you can be, a real stealthy, speedy ninja! I just hope all those years of Hulk juice kick in.

The walls are emblazoned with the afternoon sun humidifying the room. Outside the dojang, the world moves through the rice-paper walls in shadows and I feel like a shadow myself. But in the dojang everything is focused, clear and aware. I feel so alive.

Jackson and I have been kneeling for a while, breathing deeply and speaking to our hearts to practise slowing down the beats to a gentle strum. Jackson's lips twitch as he ponders for a moment, then suddenly he yells, 'Catch this!'

He spears his body towards the ceiling and spins once, sending a spinning hook kick to graze past my nose. I catch his heel mid-kick and pin it to the ground. His body lands hard against the mats and I twist his leg into a submission hold. We are so close and I blush.

'Caught it,' I say. To cover my embarrassment, I add, 'What type of ancient warriors are we talking about in the cemetery?'

I release him so he can answer.

'There's Hanzo, head of the ninja clans. He will test your focus,' he says. 'He has a shield across his mouth and black skin around his eyes that melts into his *shinobi shozoku*. He's the grossest thing imaginable.'

He throws a kick, but I jump, land the sole of my foot on his ankle and stamp down. He throws a right kick; I leap and stomp it down. He kicks again, this time a double front kick, and I leap into the air, land with both feet on top of his and stamp him back to the ground. He tries again and again, but every time I am too quick, my foot blocking his next move.

Jackson grabs my ponytail from behind. I spin under his arm, brushing my nose against his wrist, and come out the other side next to his elbow, where I strike, with my hand in a Y-formation, the side of his neck. He ducks, hooks the heel of my foot with his palm so I crash back onto my coccyx, then, holding firmly onto my heel with his right hand, he runs his left hand down my leg and jars my kneecap. I pretend to be in pain, then draw my knees back to my chest and explode my heels into his chest. He flies backwards, then lands, only to rebound in the air and charge back towards me. As he approaches, I reach for his ears with my feet, clamp his cheeks with my ankles, as I saw him do to Private Lincoln, twist my hips and flip him. He spins four times and lands on his feet.

'Not bad,' he says.

A 'not bad' feels like a 'totally awesome' coming from him.

I jump to my feet without using my hands. Jackson and I stalk each other, circling the mats. Sabo watches and cracks a smile.

Jackson screams, 'Ay-yah!' and rushes me with a flying side kick. I roll my chin backwards as he flies over me, the heel of his foot skimming past my chin, just missing my nose as I backbend and touch the floor with my hand. When he has passed, I straighten up again.

'Who else?' I ask.

'Shaolin Monk, master of Kung Fu, will test your movements,' he says.

Sabo flings us our ninja stars and we flick them out into the dojang and start chasing them like furious fireflies. Jackson flicks his and I chase it, then I flick my star and he flies after it. I can already tell that star chasey is going to be one of my favourite games. The ninja stars fly into the ceiling and we hook kick after them, with a triple spinning kick, tapping them with our toes and propelling them in any direction our feet choose. We strike and block each other's stars. Then we race the stars, spinning them out and backflipping across the room to beat them. I win.

'That it?' I ask, panting.

'Nope. The Apache Warrior will test your invisibility, then comes the finale.' Jackson pauses to suck in air. 'The Gladiator is the last warrior and he will test your weaponry.'

Four warriors, four tests. A bit much for any ninja-in-training, let alone me. I swallow hard.

'Speaking of weaponry,' Jackson says, sinking into a deep tiger stance double knife-hand strike, 'that's what the Tiger Scroll of Fire is all about.'

'Why fire?'

'The ancient Two Sword School that trained the first ninjas referred to combat as fire,' he says. 'The samurai traditionally only use the sword, but the ninjas ...'

'The ninjas' weapons are everything that exists,' I finish his sentence, copying his long stance, upper block, horse-riding stance, mountain block, flick of the hair.

Sabo brings over two *katana* swords. Jackson takes the one with a black leather handle and I take the one with the red leather handle. The blade is shorter than that of a typical samurai sword.

'Shorter blade for increased mobility. You wear it on your back with the hilt over the shoulder,' Jackson says, demonstrating. I copy him.

'The sword can be used in five ways,' he says.

He takes me to the wall, leans the sword, hilt up, against it and uses the guard, the *tsuba*, as a step to launch himself up onto a ceiling rafter. Then he pulls the sword up via the *sageo*, a cord attached to the scabbard, which he's tied around his ankle.

'For example, climbing,' he says, opening his arms in a 'ta-dah' action.

I lean my sword up against the wall and step up onto it, but it slips and I fall. My ego bruises.

'Again.' Jackson laughs.

Sabo offers me a hand and, with his help, I step up onto the sword and struggle onto the beam. But I forgot to tie the *sageo* around my ankle, so Sabo has to pass the sword up to me. Could I be more hopeless?

Jackson motions me to step back. He grips the sword's hilt in one hand and its scabbard in the other. He hesitates, then draws the sword out of the scabbard. A cloud of something explodes into my eyes — burning like shampoo, chlorine. 'What the —?!' I scream, struggling to keep my balance on the rafter.

'It's a combination of metal shavings, pepper and sand,' Jackson says proudly. 'Works a charm.'

'I can't see!' I yell as the world bombards me with jagged flashes of orange and green.

'The sword can be used for climbing, as a blinding device, as a probe for exploring ahead in the dark,' Jackson says, counting them off on his fingers. 'In combat, of course, against single or multiple assailants — whirl it around in a circle holding the *sageo* and you'll increase its reach.' He pauses for a moment, then adds, 'Oh, I forgot you can use the tube as a blowpipe, or a snorkel for water-based missions.'

'How could you forget that one?' I mutter, squinting at him through puffy eyelids as I shake my hair over my eyes to hide them from the glare of light.

Jackson leaps off the rafter and lands in the centre of the dojang, where he collects his ninja stars. I follow, stumbling as I land. I'm still acclimatising to the traditional two-toed *tabi* that are like sock shoes and can put you a bit off balance if you're not used to webbed feet. I'm also still half-blind.

'Beats capsicum spray,' Jackson assures me when I complain. He hands me a utility belt to tie around my waist. It contains a bamboo tube filled with gunpowder, metal shavings and pepper; a medicine canister with various compartments for herbs and poisons; a pen and pad for gathering intelligence; and a rope with a grappling hook at one end for climbing, which can also be used as a weapon for dragging people off their feet or off walls. I don't know where I'm going to meet these people who will need to be captured or hurt, but Jackson tells me that 'a ninja's enemies are everywhere'.

He hands me my ninja star, also known as a *shuriken*, meaning 'hand hidden blade'. 'There are 350 types of *shuriken*, from the traditional needle-like blades to more modern shapes. There's the cross, star or triangle with swivelling blades that unfold from two points to four, six, eight, twelve,' he says.

'Talk about ninja accessories,' I say. How am I going to learn all this in time? What if I get transported before I'm ready?

He laughs. 'You don't have to learn them all; you only have to remember. It's in your blood. Instinct.'

In the dusty light of the dojang, we advance to

other projectile weapons in the ninja armoury, such as the travel bow, a hinged bow that can be folded into a walking stick to avoid detection. Jackson shows me how to make an emergency bow out of bamboo. I feel nervous as we sit cross-legged in our uniforms carving the bows. Elecktra is the artistic one.

'Do you know how to make your own arrows too?' I ask.

'Yep,' he says.

Jackson stands and walks over to a chest of drawers in the corner of the dojang. His scent of freshly washed clothes and home-made pasta sauce follows him; I get a whiff and smile happily. He takes out a tray of miniature arrows.

'These are some I prepared earlier,' he says. 'Poison-tipped.'

'But they're so little.'

'They can be shot from a tiny bow, or out of a blowpipe made from a short length of bamboo, or even a simple roll of paper from your notebook,' he tells me.

'Wow,' I say, studying the tiny needles.

'Spitting needles have been around long before Hero started using them at Gate Two,' he says. 'This is how ninjas used to communicate. They used the darts to send messages — to get intelligence to besieged forces inside a village, for instance.'

My heart sinks at the mention of Gate Two. In the dojang, I feel capable and strong, but when I step outside I am myself again. Gate Two Roxy.

I step closer to Jackson and tilt my head for a passing breeze of his smell. But, as always, as soon as I get close, he steps back. The only time he really touches me is when we're fighting. I know I'm far too young for love combat. But I can't help it!

'Ninjas think of everything,' I say. Everything but love.

FOURTEEN

Sergeant Major calls Years Seven to Ten out of normal classes for a special fitness test. The other teachers obviously aren't happy, but there is a big focus on sport and fitness at Hindley Hall. This was one of the reasons Mum chose the school for Elecktra and me, particularly when she met Sergeant Major at the school open day and was impressed with his army training and emphasis on fitness and discipline.

Sergeant Major lines us all up on the oval. 'Side line side,' he commands.

We look left and raise a straight arm to the shoulder of the person next to us.

'Straight arms. Look right. Straight line!' Sergeant Major yells.

We shuffle again as kids push in.

'Not fast enough. Squats!' Sergeant Major yells.

We put our hands on our heads and begin a series of squats. The 'groaners', as Sergeant Major calls them, are instructed to do it double time. We count forty squats in unison. Sergeant Major blows his whistle and we stop.

'Side line side!' he yells again, and this time we make the formation in twenty seconds. He clicks his boots together in approval. We stand at attention, hands in fists by our sides, staring into the distance.

'Today is a simple fitness test,' he says. 'To see who is fit, who is fast, who can evade, dodge, defend and stand their ground. And you will all show me this with a simple game of Tiggy.' He smiles. The older kids groan. I can tell Year Seven is excited. Tiggy is our speciality.

We are instructed to split into groups of ten. The aim is to tag as many kids in your team as possible. If you get tapped on the shoulder, you are out.

'The last person standing will be the winner,' Sergeant Major says.

Elecktra and Jackson are way down the line, but I can hear Elecktra giggling. That gaping hole in my heart becomes a canyon. Jackson knows Elecktra is my sister. What if he likes her more than me?

To make it more challenging Sergeant Major divides us into groups that contain a mix of older and younger students. I can't believe it when he puts Hero, Bruce and Krew with Cinnamon, Jackson, Elecktra and me.

'Ready ready,' Sergeant Major calls.

The game starts and we are all sprinting in different

directions; it's already total madness. My heart is bursting after a few minutes of trying to keep out of everyone's way. Elecktra is running after Jackson, but he's too quick for her. He catches my eye and folds his hands into the water sign. Even from across the oval, I see his moss-green eyes wink at me and I know he hasn't forgotten about me — yet. I understand his message. My mission is no longer just to tag other kids. This is a ninja training session.

I pause and close my eyes, then fold my hands into the water symbol representing the Water Tiger Scroll: left palm pointing up to my chin in prayer position, right hand making a fist and held an eyelash distance from the left palm. I feel the strong rock of my right hand and the fluidity of my left palm pushing against it to create a magnetic force that keeps my mind clear, my breathing deep and my body motionless. I feel myself lift slightly off the ground. I let my mind unload beneath me, shedding all the things that have been weighing me down: Hero's threats, Mum's attack and then her departure, Elecktra not wanting to know me at school and trying to take Jackson for herself, not knowing who my father is or what to do about my powers. The power of water runs through me. The invisible streams erode old beliefs like rocks and nourish new thoughts like trees.

In a single moment I am no longer the awkward kid who never says the right thing or wears the right clothes. I am me, Roxy Ran, thirteen-year-old ninja-in-training. And that is more than enough. Like an orchid, I blossom. All those hang-ups rinse out of my skin and soak deep into the grass.

When I feel as light as a ninja star, I open my eyes and bring my hand up to my face. Nothing. I look down to my toes and again, nothing. For the first time, I am completely invisible.

I look over at Jackson and he is smiling through me. Hero runs past Jackson and slaps him on the shoulder. Jackson is out of the game, but exits with a smile.

Sergeant Major sends more kids into the game and the oval is chaos, with kids running into each other. It's easy for me to flash invisible without being noticed. Everyone is too busy saving themselves to see what I'm up to.

Cinnamon and Lecky are out, leaving me against Hero, Bruce and Krew, who are spread out across the oval, ready to capture me. I manage to creep up behind Krew, flash visible at the last second and then slap him on the shoulder without the others noticing. Krew jumps, his pin eyes expanding to walnuts when he realises it's me.

Still visible, I run to the other side of the oval. Bruce has his hands on his knees and is panting. I cruise up behind him, hiding myself from the rest of the class, then flash invisible and slap him on the shoulder.

'What the —?' he says, looking around and seeing no one is there. I flash visible and smile like a Cheshire cat. He is furious.

'Out,' Sergeant Major calls and Bruce storms off.

Now it's only Hero and me left. He charges after me. He's so fast it's as if his feet don't touch the ground, as though he's levitating, dragging his toes through the air. I can't flash invisible now; it would be too risky with all the other kids watching. I must rely on my other super power — courage. It's the hardest to muster. I run as fast as I can, hearing Hero gain on me and feeling the wind of his chase through my hair. I can't run forever. I decide to surprise attack. I stop, turn and somersault towards him. He isn't expecting me to dive low, and before he can screech to a stop, I smack him on the shoe. Tagged!

'Roxy wins,' Sergeant Major calls across the oval. 'Well done.'

As we're all trooping back to class, Jackson comes up and whispers in my ear, 'Pretty impressive, Roxy Rox.'

My cheeks heat at the compliment and I think, *I am ninja*. When I gaze after him, I see Hero staring at me with evil in his eyes.

The next day, I cruise through Gate Two unscathed. Are the bullies having a day off? I'm deep in thought when I hear cheering and spy a congregation of Gate One kids in front of the mansion. I shove my way through the crowd. In the middle of the circle, Hero is holding Jackson in a headlock. Cinnamon is cowering on the sideline. Elecktra is standing behind Cinnamon's afro, hiding.

'Say it!' Hero demands, gripping Jackson's throat tighter in the crook of his elbow. His knees are bent and you can see every joint in his body applying pressure to Jackson's neck.

'Jackson!' I yell.

Hero looks up. The veins in his forehead snake into his temples with the pressure of the hold. He smiles when he sees me. Jackson is grunting and trying to breathe.

'Say Roxy Ran is a total loser!' Hero yells.

Kids are closing in around us, chanting and cheering Hero on. I am drowned in the centre of the circle. The world shrinks to a hurricane of sneers and insults. All I can smell is BO. The antiseptic taste of fear soaks into my mouth. Usually in a situation like this, I'd wish to disappear, but that won't stop Hero hurting Jackson.

'Say it!' Hero jolts Jackson's neck violently.

Jackson shakes his head, grunts, stamps his foot, then yells with all his might, 'You're a total loser!' He heaves another breath. 'I used to beat you in comp and always will.'

Hero's face drains of colour. He wouldn't want people knowing he'd ever been beaten in competition.

144

Less glory for his trophy locker. He growls and pushes Jackson away, knocking him to the ground. I help him up. His nose is bleeding.

The circle closes in, kids are shouting.

'You know you want to,' Hero sneers. 'Say Roxy is a loser!'

Jackson stands tall and looks at Hero from under a bloodied brow. 'No,' he says.

Hero takes a step backwards, winds back his arm and pushes Jackson. Jackson falls backwards. He hits the concrete.

I want to take Hero on, but the jeering crowd and the power of him make me lose my ninja nerve. I turn away from Hero and bend down to help Jackson up again.

'Pizza,' someone calls and the crowd disperses. What is it with these guys and pizza?

Jackson looks pretty dazed and I feel completely responsible.

'You should have just said it,' I whisper.

'No, I couldn't,' he says. 'So, you coming to the dojang later?'

He sure is persistent. Persistently crazy.

I have something to finish before I go to the dojang after school. I race home and burst into Elecktra's bedroom.

'Why didn't you stand up for me today?' I yell. 'Jackson could have been really hurt!'

Elecktra is combing her hair at her dressing table.

'I'm thinking of running for Deputy School Captain,' she says.

I walk over to the dressing table and snatch her brush in my hand.

'Ouch!' she screams.

'Not ouch,' I say. 'Ouch is having everyone chanting awful things about you and seeing your older sister hiding behind your best friend's hair. Ouch is having a new kid, who's known you five minutes, get pushed around while your sister, who's known you your whole life, just stands there.' I lean in closer. 'Ouch is knowing that I would do anything for you, Lecky, and you don't care one bit about me.' I let go of her brush.

Elecktra stares at me, her dark eyes oiling with tears. 'Cat, you've never yelled at me like that before,' she stammers. Her bottom lip quivers.

I choose not to stay for the drama. 'Oh, stop fake crying,' I say and slam her door behind me.

I've been hanging out for today's lesson on fire training, *kaki*. Since the dojang sits behind an abandoned petrol station, Sabo suggested we drive to a nearby deserted quarry to practise. Jackson's brought the gunpowder and wants to show me how to handle fire safely. It'll also be useful for when I go to the Cemetery of Warriors. Samurai are famous for their predilection for fire.

Sabo sets up a fold-out chair, rests a fire extinguisher underneath it, takes a sports drink out of his Esky and sits down to read the paper. His Taekwondo uniform works as a suntan reflector, beaming rays up into his face. He puts on his sunglasses. He doesn't need to tell us to be careful as Jackson has done so much fire training.

'You haven't said much about the Cemetery of Warriors lately,' I say to Jackson as he sets up the explosives. He has a black eye from Hero. The dark bruising under his eye makes the green flecks flicker.

He shrugs. 'The warriors are there to protect their lineage and the purity of their fighting art.'

Suddenly, I'm seized by panic. I can't defend myself against any kind of warrior! I'm a newbie ninja — hardly a ninja at all. I still can't throw my ninja star straight, and my strikes and kicks need more work. How am I meant to defeat a master?

I grip Jackson by the shoulders and shake him. 'What if I can't do it?'

'It's just one move at a time,' he says, calmly removing my hands and placing them in a prayer meditation position.

'Stop speaking in bumper stickers,' I say. 'I could die!' Why does he believe in me so much when no one else does?

Jackson fetches a carton of pre-prepared hollowed-out eggs from the van. He uses a straw to blow some gunpowder into an egg, then throws it to the ground at his feet. Nothing happens. He tries again with another egg. Still nothing happens.

'The gunpowder's meant to make an explosion,' he says, 'and I would vanish behind the smoke screen.'

'And?' I say, hands on hips.

I roll my eyes as he tries and fails for a third time to make himself vanish with an egg.

We move on to attaching gunpowder-filled paper tubes to arrows, which we shoot at trees. Every time Jackson hits the target, Sabo cheers.

'Usually we'd aim for flammable surfaces,' Jackson tells me.

I aim at the tree, pull back my elbow and release the arrow. It shoots backwards, not forwards, and pierces the soil close to Sabo's feet.

'Watch it, girl!' Sabo yells as a small fire emerges. 'My eyebrows are a feature — I'd like to keep them.' He fans the drifting smoke away from his face and throws his sports drink on the flames.

'Sooo, I hear you've been hanging around with my sister, Elecktra,' I say as we practise with the arrows.

'Yeah. Elecktra's cool,' he replies.

My heart shrinks to a pin. It has taken some bravery for me to mention this and it wasn't the response I wanted to hear.

'She's super cool,' he adds.

In boy language this translates to 'super cute'. I throw down my bow and arrows and storm off into the bushes. Jackson catches up with me and spins me around.

'You still think she's super cool, even though she didn't stick up for me?' I search the green horizons of his eyes.

'I know, I'm being pathetic,' Jackson says.

'And I'm pathetic at being a ninja,' I sigh.

'No.' He puts a hand on my shoulder and I feel lighter than I do when I flash invisible. 'You're learning.'

'But I can't fire arrows. My weaponry is lame. I'll never get to the Cemetery of Warriors at this rate,' I say, kicking rocks with my *tabi*.

Jackson takes five steps backwards, then shoots an arrow into a tree trunk directly above my head. It's a perfect shot.

'Bow and arrow was my weakest weapon too,' he says. He takes my hand and the world colours again. 'Don't give up, okay?' He smiles. 'Friends?'

I squeeze his hand, and he squeezes it back.

We return to the training and I learn how to twirl fire sticks with sharpened points at either end, and scrunch gunpowder balls of paper that can be thrown like bombs. They remind me of the brown-paper fertiliser bombs kids use on frenemies' doorsteps. When you stamp on them to put out the fire, you step in the fertiliser. Disgusting!

Although I'm still pretty hopeless at the bow and arrow, I manage to master the *torinoke* — the eggs blown with gunpowder that create a smoke screen for disappearing. Jackson is very impressed. After I've vanished several times, we move on to specialised weapons, such as the chain-and-sickle weapon, which is a length of chain with a sickle-shaped blade projecting at a right angle from one end and a weight on the other. The weighted chain is used to ensnare an opponent's wrist or ankle and drag them off their feet, then the sickle finishes them off.

'These weapons come from our early origins. They were all farming tools,' Jackson says.

'How were they used for farming?' I ask.

'Don't know,' he says. 'But it sounds cool.'

I arrive home from training exhausted. Art is painting the living room a glowing iridescent yellow. He reckons Elecktra and I have been fighting a lot lately and, in our mother's absence, he is determined to calm us down with 'colour therapy'. But my gut isn't feeling it. I drag my feet up the stairs, turn the corner and stop when I see my door.

I bend down to inspect the handle and smile. My doorknob is missing and in its place is Elecktra's. She has covered it with pink rhinestones and in the centre is an encrusted sapphire R. I trace the rhinestones with my finger.

'I call it handle-dazzle,' Elecktra says behind me. 'I'm going to do Mum's too. I've already bought the gold rhinestones. I did my phone,' she says and flashes her phone at me. It's covered in multicoloured stones.

I continue to inspect the doorknob. It must have taken her ages, the stones are set perfectly.

'Cat, I've been so stressed. My stomach is bloated. I hate it when we don't talk.' She casts her eyes down. I notice that she's wearing her school tie around her wrist in a bow. 'Are we friends?' she asks.

I look at the doorknob, then at Elecktra's pleading eyes. I can't shake the memory of her hiding behind Cinnamon's hair while Hero called me names.

'Lecky, I don't want to be friends,' I say and open my door. 'I want to be sisters.'

I close my door and hear her storm off.

'Well, that was a waste of sparkles!' she yells.

FIFTEEN

The only ninja skill I'm really good at is being invisible.
Go figure. Invisibility magic could come in handy —
imagine all the things I'll be able to do! Spy on my
classmates, my parents, Lecky, read my report card early.
The possibilities are endless!

The next day at school, I can't resist any longer. I
follow Elecktra and Jackson into the boys' locker room.
The place is deserted and filled with forgotten sports gear.

'It smells disgusting in here,' Elecktra says.

Jackson laughs. Why is he laughing at that?

Elecktra takes Jackson's hand and pulls him towards
her. He doesn't put up a fight.

Elecktra giggles.

My ears explode!

Don't fall for this! I scream at him in my mind. I feel
my stomach turn to barbed wire, my mouth fills with
sand. I can't swallow or breathe. Just the one thought
over and over: *I saw him first. He's my friend.*

I met him first. I'm training to be a ninja. He's my instructor. Elecktra has everything already — beauty, popularity, straight teeth. He's the first guy who has ever even noticed me. And now she's stealing him.

I calm my mind, allow all thoughts to drain out of me and slowly turn invisible. I walk up to them, so close I can see Jackson's long eyelashes twitch. I slow my own breathing and take a piece of cotton wool out of my pocket and shove it up my nose to reduce the sound of my breathing even more.

'Roxy?' Elecktra blinks at me under the silk fans of her eyelashes. 'What are you doing here? I didn't see you come in?' she squeals.

I am standing almost between them, my cotton-wool-stuffed nose a mere centimetre from Jackson's jaw. Thinking negative thoughts caused my invisibility to fail.

Jackson shuffles his feet. He steps back from Elecktra. She moves closer.

'Go away!' she yells at me.

I can't move. Jackson still doesn't look at me.

'Scram!' she shouts.

I search his face like it's a crossword. No clue.

'I just wanted to check tonight was still on?' I say in a shaky voice.

'Yep. Sure,' he says cagily.

'What's tonight? What's going on?' Elecktra snaps.

He looks at her and then smiles kindly at me. 'I'm just helping Roxy with some homework.'

Homework. I'm helping him find the White Warrior and this is how he refers to me — as someone who needs help with their homework. I take the cotton wool out of my nose and wait for him to look at me, but his eyes are downwards.

I walk out of the locker room. I've never felt so Gate Two in my life.

'So how are things?' Jackson asks as I enter the dojang that evening after school.

'How do you think?' I snap.

He reties the knot of his belt and whips the ends tight. 'Seriously, are you okay?' he asks.

I ignore him.

'Okay. Let's start with kicks then,' he says. 'I'll need you in bare feet. Our lesson today is basic side kick, blade of the foot to the jugular.'

He shows me how to warm up my muscles, then leads me to the centre of the dojang mats, where we bow to each other and I follow him into a deep horse-riding stance. He takes one step to the right, tucks his left knee under his chin, then tilts his body back as his leg extends straight up from his hip, the blade of his sole reaching for the ceiling. Then he retracts his knee to his chin, his uniform crackling with the sharp move, and returns to horse-riding stance.

'Go,' he says.

I take a step, pull my knee up to my chin, but I lose my balance and fall down. I'm a disaster. I try again and this time manage to whip my foot out to the side.

'Blade of the foot,' Jackson repeats, 'push through the hip and then the heel.'

I try to push through the heel, but my foot hates it.

'Higher,' Jackson says.

I collapse onto the floor.

'You can do better than this,' he says.

I glare at him. 'Sorry if I'm *not* Elecktra,' I say.

'What's *she* got to do with *your* side kick?' he strikes back.

'You would never tell Elecktra she was hopeless,' I say, crossing my feet and arms.

He looks at me, bewildered by my attitude. Something about his splintering gaze annoys me. He's not paying enough attention! If I was Elecktra, those eyes would be riveted on me.

I launch at him to bring his fractured gaze back to me. He grabs my wrist as I come at him, twists me under his arm three times into a submission hold. We are chest to chest.

155

I curl my hands around his forearms and feel the hours of his ceiling push-ups and years of training, then hip-throw him over my shoulder. He break-falls and rolls back onto his feet, then stands up slowly, pulling on his bottom lip where he bit it.

'Not bad,' he says and smiles.

He launches at me with a hammer-fist overhead strike and I roll out of the way into a climbing axe kick, stepping up onto his knee for extra height and stomping my foot to the ceiling. When I land, I see him as if through a sheet of water, shimmering, perfect, a battle light in his eyes. We fight with thunderous kicks, smashing blocks, twisting arm locks, slicing *shuriken*, until we are both keening with exhaustion. We run at each other full tilt and roundhouse kick at the same time. Our legs smash together, the insteps of our feet crunching bone to bone. We both yelp and break away, hopping and clutching our feet.

'Ready to train properly now?' Jackson asks, hobbling back to the centre.

He takes my silence for a yes and tells me to sit down and lean back on my hands. Oddly, I feel much better.

'Bring your knee to your chest and extend your leg and hold,' he instructs.

I do as he says. He gently takes my right foot in his warm hands and rotates my toes so they don't point to the ceiling; rather the blade of my foot slices upwards.

'In martial arts, the foot has three positions: ball of the foot, heel of the foot and blade of the foot,' he says, showing me the different positions with delicate movements of my foot.

I'm holding my breath, hoping he doesn't notice the long brown birthmark that runs from the ball of my foot all the way across my arch to my heel.

He bends my knee back to my chin, then glides my leg forwards again and twists my foot to show the correct position.

'You're really cool, Roxy Rox,' he says. 'Like the sister I wished I had.'

How did I end up being his sister, with my own sister treating me like a distant cousin?

Suddenly, Jackson yells, 'Sabo! Quick, come here!'

Sabo shuffles over and Jackson pulls up my heel and drags me forwards.

'Look!' he says.

'Hey! Watch it!' I squeal.

Sabo and Jackson are studying the sole of my foot with their mouths open.

'It's a stupid birthmark. Sort of looks like a cat. I hate it,' I say. 'My family calls me 'Cat' as a nickname. I'm going to get it removed one day. Lasered off as soon as I'm old enough.'

They continue staring, silent, blinking.

I pull my foot away and cross my legs to hide the mark. 'Forget it,' I tell them.

'Okay, sure,' Jackson says, exchanging a look with Sabo. 'But I'd say it looks more like a tiger than a cat.'

'What? What are you saying?'

'Nothing,' he says, his eyes not meeting mine.

I try to do the side kick again, but my foot won't twist and turn the way it's meant to and my hips feel stiff from all the training. My whole body aches.

'Forget side kicks.' Jackson pulls me to my feet. 'Come with me,' he says.

Jackson takes me over to the wall of silver rings.

'I didn't know there was a ninja jewellery line,' I joke, taking down a claw ring and putting it on my finger. I hold my hand out, as I've seen women do to show off their engagement rings.

'Not jewellery,' he says. 'They're knuckledusters, hand claws, finger spikes and hooks.' He slips a hand claw over his wrist; the claws extend thirty centimetres past his fingers. 'Used for slapping, punching, climbing,' he says. 'You can deflect a sword blade with your hands, or use the claws to catch the blade to twist or break it.'

'But I bet there is a girl you'd like to give a ring to,' I hint.

He looks at me, confused. 'These are lethal weapons, Roxy. You have to take them seriously.'

I mimic his serious face. 'Who taught you all this stuff anyway?'

'My mother. She was killed by a samurai when I was young,' he replies, opening and closing his fingers so the claws extend sharply and retract.

I wait for a flash of emotion. But there's nothing. A fog of awkwardness settles around us.

'I'm sorry,' I say and look away. The thought of my own mother being dead is too hard to imagine. She's still away on her work trip and I miss her so much.

Jackson selects a gleaming silver ring with a spike from the wall and slides it onto my finger. I watch him fiddle with the ring on my finger until the awkwardness evaporates.

'The horn ring is the preferred weapon of female ninjas,' he tells me. 'Dip the end in poison and you're good to go.'

I stare at the horn ring. It is the most beautiful thing I've ever seen. In my crazy imagination, the man of my dreams bends down on one knee and presents me with a red velvet box. I open the box, tears trickling down my face, and inside is a diamond horn ring. I accept his proposal immediately ...

'The finger spikes are used to target pressure points,' Jackson says, tearing me from my daydream.

I needle the ring into the side of his neck to test it.

'Hey, that hurts, Fancy Face!' he yells.

He hasn't called me that recently. An inner warmth starts to glow.

We practise walking along the dojang walls using the horn rings.

Jackson introduces me to toe claws next.

'What are these for?' I ask.

'The upside-down crawl,' he says. 'Ninja ceiling push-ups.'

'You're joking.'

Jackson flings himself up the wall, climbing knee to wrist and keeping low until he reaches the top. When he meets the ceiling, he turns sharply and lies flat against it, hooking the toe claws into his ninja slippers. When the climbing claws are in place, he shifts his weight and uses them as footholds, lying still and silent, waiting for his enemy to walk beneath so he can drop on them like a black spider.

'That's ninja!' I call up to him.

I launch up the wall with my own toe claws, but when I make a sharp turn as Jackson did to lie on the ceiling, I plummet back down to crash-land on the padded martial arts mats. Jackson laughs. He triple-spins off the roof and lands in front of me in crouching-tiger stance.

'We'll work on that,' he says. 'When you've mastered all fourteen ninja principles, the ceiling climb will get easier.'

'I need a set of biceps,' I say.

He squeezes my arm playfully. 'I think your arms are pretty good the way they are.'

Here we go again — more blushing from me.

After climbing training, we move on to walking training. Walking ninja ranges from small stabbing steps to creeping through leaf litter and shallow water. Jackson pours water onto the mats so I can practise the skating movements of sideways walking through narrow corridors or staying tight to a wall to avoid detection. Next are the running and sweeping steps, where I learn to transfer my weight gently from one foot to the other.

Finally, Jackson covers the dojang floor with sheets of paper.

'If you make a noise, you have to start again,' he instructs.

The paper crackles beneath me on my first stabbing step. 'This is impossible,' I say.

'Only if you think it's impossible.' He runs the full length of the paper without making a sound.

I practise my short stabbing steps, then sweeping steps and side-stepping steps until it gets dark.

'We'll have to wait to progress to the bamboo balancing,' Jackson tells Sabo, who has been watching us.

Sabo agrees that if I can't walk ninja yet, there's no way I'll be able to balance ninja-style.

My heart sinks. I'm as hopeless at walking just as much as I was the bow and arrow. Those cemetery warriors are going to slaughter me. That is, if Hero doesn't get to me first.

I follow Jackson outside, where a bamboo rope ladder with iron grappling hooks at the top end drapes over the dojang roof. Jackson races up the ladder with one foot on each rung. I climb the ladder with two feet on each rung, like a nanna. Still in bare feet, we walk across the roof to the back of the building, where the city lights are blinking in the twilight.

'Jump,' Jackson says.

'Are you crazy?'

'Are you a ninja?'

'I don't know,' I say, looking over the edge at the drop of six or seven metres. 'I can't. I'll kill myself.'

'Trust me. You can jump from here to that rooftop over there.' He points to a roof at least half a kilometre away.

'That's not jumping, that's flying! That rooftop's practically in another state.'

I've done this before, twice, but the first time I was being chased by my mother with a sword and didn't have time to think, and the second I had Cinnamon to balance me out and we were only leaping over small gaps, not canyons like this!

'Fine,' he says. 'Let's forget flying and go back to the side kick. Balance on one leg, tuck your knee to your chin and hold,' he instructs, walking behind me.

I do as he says, grateful he's moved on. The smell of pasta sauce wafts up as Jackson moves closer.

'Now extend your leg up into a blade of the foot side kick,' he says.

I tilt my body and extend my leg up into the sky. My legs side-split easily this time, and I lock on my core to hold the position. After thirty seconds of holding my balance, I've heard nothing from Jackson. I pivot slightly on my supporting leg so I can see him. He's on the other side of the building.

'What are you doing over there?' I call.

'Teaching you how to fly!' he yells back, then launches into a sweeping step run. I don't even have time to retract my kick before he pushes me and I plunge forwards off the building, screaming.

But then something magical happens. My body doesn't fall but keeps propelling higher, my legs extend out into the splits, my toes reaching. My hair billows behind me and it's as if every strand is thrusting me forwards. I glide through the air and land in a forward roll on the roof of the next building. I slowly stand up. Shocked. Was that another fluke? I think the trick is not to think about it.

'You just flew! A very long way!' Jackson yells, waving at me. He turns and walks down the side of the dojang with his climbing claws wedged between his toes. 'See ya back there,' he calls.

'How?' I call back.

'Fly like before.'

He makes it sound so easy. Like 'walk' or 'run'.

After a while, the sky has washed to darkness and I'm still on the roof. In the moonlight, I study the birthmark on my sole. Jackson called it a tiger. The tiger's tail curls around my heel and he's leaping across my arch, his hind legs extended across my heel and his front paws reaching into my toes. You can see his snarly mouth and whiskers.

I plant my foot down, walk to the back of the building, take a deep breath and fill my mind with birds, wind, feathers, light. Then I run in sweeping steps as fast as I can. I have only one thought: *Fly, tiger, fly.*

I feel my muscles contract as I crouch before the launch, then my legs twitch and release into an effortless split position, stretching higher and further.

Every molecule of my being is extended and flexible. I feel the wind behind me, gusting me forwards, and I clear my mind of all thoughts of doubt and negativity. I focus on landing safely on the roof of the dojang. This time, I turn the forward roll into a tiger stance followed by a triple side kick, with a yelled, 'Ay-yah!'

There is no one here to witness my little victory, but sometimes the best wins are those that mean the most only to you. I punch the air in celebration. Now I know I'll be able to go the 'top way' to school every day. No more Gate Two for me.

SIXTEEN

A warm breath against my neck wakes me from my sleep. I sit up and scream. There are three samurai around my bed with long swords pointed at my heart. They are wearing ruby silk kimonos, with a long piece of metal armour down the front of the body and tied around the front with a metal chain. Despite the clothes, and the shadows that distort their features, I recognise them: Hero, Krew and Bruce. Their eyes are bloodshot with evil.

'What do you want?' I say, my voice trembling.

Hero scrapes his blade up to my shoulder. 'I wish I could kill you,' he sneers. 'But it's against the Bushido code to take vengeance that is not your own.' His breath smells like sour milk.

I truly don't know what he's talking about. Is this a nightmare? What vengeance?

'I don't know where the White Warrior is,' I finally say.

As soon as the words leave my mouth, Hero applies pressure to his sword. If I move, even breathe, the steel will pierce me.

'You've got to train hard to be transported to the Cemetery of Warriors,' he says. 'I've been training my whole life for it. I'll find the White Warrior first. Stay out of it!'

'The White Warrior should be protected, not destroyed,' I say.

He jabs his blade into my shoulder. 'Says who?'

'But you'll start a clan war!' I say.

His sword presses deeper and I feel it nick my skin. The pain needles to a single pulsating spot like a bee sting. This is no dream. Their swords are as real as my mother's sword was when she ran across the rooftops.

'No more words, filthy ninja?' Hero taunts.

It takes the strength of every cell in my body to fake courage. 'If I'd known I was going to have company, I would have worn different pyjamas,' I say. Pink ponies and the slogan 'Hot to trot' aren't exactly threatening.

Hero grinds his teeth with anger. He looks at Bruce and Krew and nods. The three of them run out of my room.

I race after them and find them in Elecktra's bedroom, their swords at her long throat. Elecktra continues to dream; her rosebud lips seem to exhale perfume.

'Maybe I should just kill your sister instead,' Hero sneers.

'No!' I whisper.

Hero thrusts his sword towards Elecktra's heart and I scream.

Elecktra wakes. 'What the heck is going on?' she yells, jumping out of bed. 'Are you spying on me?'

Hero and his clan have disappeared out the window.

'No,' I say, searching desperately for a cover story. 'I was having a nightmare. And with Mum gone, I thought ...'

'Fat chance, Roxy,' she says. 'Go back to bed. Go on!'

I leave Elecktra's room feeling sick. The world's deadliest teenager just threatened to kill my sister.

I creep downstairs to the kitchen for a glass of milk to calm me down. My heart feels like a pair of cymbals and won't let me rest. I can still feel Hero's breath on my neck, his sword stinging my shoulder. I almost feel paralysed with fear. I heat up some milk in the microwave, then sit on a stool to slowly sip the comforting drink.

I smooth my hand across the wood of the table. I feel every groove of the boats' journeys beneath my fingertips: the storms, the loneliness, the infinite horizon. I sympathise with them — being lost at sea must be similar to how I feel now. My palm glides across the slats: dark mahogany merged with bright maple; elm, oak and cedar parallel strips — all so different and yet forged together, a bit like Elecktra and me. My favourite part of the table sits under the coral-shaped bowl. The wood came from a boat that must have been repainted hundreds of times — it's turquoise with brushings of pink and sapphire.

I close my eyes and sail my fingers over its grooves, inhaling the resin scent that sparks memories of fires in winter and toasted marshmallows. I flick my eyes open suddenly and lean in. There's a smooth patch on the table that I've never noticed before: a piece of sandalwood in a slice of mahogany. I rub it with my thumb and hear a clicking sound, like the opening of a lock. I press down on it and the table breaks apart at the centre. I push my stool back in shock as the table pieces widen automatically and a shelf rises to the top where the coral bowl usually sits. On it is a small black book. I stand motionless, in disbelief.

Moonlight spears through the skylight, emblazoning the gold writing on the book's jacket. Hesitantly, I reach out a single finger to touch the book's surface. Nothing happens. I climb back up on one of the face stools and peer down at the writing. Staring at me, it reads:

AS A NINJA,
MY BODY IS A WEAPON,
MY MOVEMENTS ARE MAGICAL,
MY FOCUS IS LETHAL.
I AM THE INVISIBLE WARRIOR.

I pluck the book from the shelf and hold it in my hands. It feels weightless, even though my fingertips touch the solid heaviness of leather. I open the book to the first page, but it isn't a book at all. It is empty inside and filled with five tiny white scrolls held by fine gold rods. The scrolls are the size of shortbread finger biscuits; the paper translucent. I can just decipher silver glowing script on the scrolls. I touch one and it feels like water. When I pull my finger away, it is wet. I put my finger in my mouth and it tastes like water with cherry blossom in it.

Freaked out, I shut the book and put it back on the shelf. I press the sandalwood panel and the table moves back together. I slide the coral-shaped bowl over the wood, then stare at it to think.

At lunchtime the next day, I find Jackson in the library, near the atlases, where we agreed to meet. I dig into my bag, pull out the black book and hand it over.

He takes it without breaking eye contact. The washing machine in my stomach starts churning.

'Look inside,' I say.

He slides down the bookshelf and sits on the floor with his legs apart, then places the book delicately between them. He floats his hand over its surface and silently recites the ninja creed on the cover. I watch his lips move.

'Wow, I'm nervous.' He looks up at me and laughs. 'I've been waiting so long for this.'

I crouch down next to him. 'I'm nervous too,' I say.

He gazes at me for what feels like a very long time. My heart balloons. I lean in, close my eyes, then the air flattens between us.

Jackson slaps the book. 'I can't believe you found the Tiger Scrolls!' he says, triumphantly holding the book up between us.

I stand up, my cheeks blistering with confusion. I bury my face in an atlas.

'Where were they?' he asks.

I shrug. 'In the kitchen table.'

I slowly pull my hair behind my ear. He's acting as if nothing happened. Did something just happen? Something did happen. I felt it. I'm sure of it.

'Okay, I'm ready,' he says. As he slowly opens the book, a white light shines into his face, making his eyes glow.

'They're so cute!' he exclaims.

I crouch down next to him again. His use of the word 'cute' just made him even more irresistible. Now I have a bigger problem than dealing with Hero. Do I want to train as a ninja to help find the White Warrior, or just to be closer to Jackson?

'They look like biscuits,' I agree, only just managing to keep the confused hurt from my voice.

I gesture for him to pick up one of the scrolls. He does so, carefully, then drops it and sucks on his finger.

'Hot,' he says, shaking his hand.

'I touched one and it was wet,' I say. 'I think each one feels like the element it represents.'

He closes the book and looks around the library, then signals me closer. I don't make the mistake of closing my eyes this time.

'Keep these on you at all times,' he says. 'And don't let anyone see them!'

SEVENTEEN

Dawdling to class, the scrolls tucked away in my school bag, I'm brushed by Cinnamon's wild hair blazing past me. In her hands is a phone. She's running and that girl rarely runs. This must be important. I sprint after her down the corridor. 'Cim!' I call. But her hair is an engine propelling her forwards and not even I can catch her in the crowded hallway.

She races into the classroom and plugs the phone into the interactive whiteboard cable.

'What are you doing?' I say, panting in the doorway. Her fingers are frantic. Who knew she could move like a ginger ninja?

'I'm on a mission,' she says, her sweating skin glistening like strawberry lip gloss. She waits for the video to download to the laptop, then clicks it open. The video flashes up onto the whiteboard.

'What's that?'

'Between me and Jackson,' she says and winks, just as Jackson would. 'You'll see.'

She floats the mouse over the Play button and licks her cherry lips. I've never seen her this confident. Kids begin to shuffle to their desks, dragging their feet.

'Sit,' Cinnamon commands me.

The strength in her voice pulls me down. 'Yes, ma'am,' I say, and sit with my knees together and back straight.

Hero and his friends are last to come in. His eyes narrow on Cinnamon sitting upright in the front row and he starts the usual insults. 'Cinnamon donut,' he sneers. 'And Poxy Roxy, with a face like smashed crabs.'

Cinnamon's eyes steel against Hero's venom. There isn't a glimmer of a tear or a tremor of her Adam's apple. Her hair is a rumpled red mess, but for the first time I see his taunts bounce off it rather than soak in.

I watch the cursor hover above the Play button, waiting. What is she up to? Her eyes are fierce. She is battle ready.

'Cinnamon donut!' Hero shouts again.

Other kids join in his laughter, and murmurs and smirks follow.

Cinnamon smiles and her cheeks become toffee apples. She swivels to the class. 'Quiet!' she bellows.

Most people hush, some kids giggle.

'I've prepared a treat for you all,' she says and turns back around to face the whiteboard.

The class simmers with intrigue.

I stare at her. 'Who are you? And what have you done with my best friend?' I murmur.

Cinnamon takes a last look at me, then turns to the laptop and clicks Play. I move to the edge of my seat, as nervous as the first time I entered the dojang.

Hero flashes up on screen. The class silences immediately.

He is holding Rescue over the toilet bowl. 'I hate ferrets,' he says and drops the kitten into the bowl. The kitten squeals.

The girls in the class scream — they're all big fans of Rescue. Cinnamon has been letting them visit him in her locker for cuddles and he has become something of a school mascot.

A soundtrack cuts in and I explode onto the screen, blasting Hero with kicks and strikes. I slide down in my chair and pull my hair over my face, trying to hide my pulsating red cheeks. Hero is going to murder me.

The video shows Hero and me fighting; first I win, then Hero is winning. Then Bruce and Krew get involved, and all the while Rescue is drowning. The class begins cheering for me. On screen, I seem to fight harder.

'Go, Roxy!' someone yells out.

I sit up and brush some hair off my face. I find the courage to look at Cinnamon, who is shadow-boxing the screen, mimicking my fight moves.

I suddenly remember that Jackson was in the toilet cubicle that day. He must have filmed the fight on his phone.

As I race across the screen and save Rescue from drowning, the class cheers and hollers. My front-row neighbour leans over and slaps me on the back. Cinnamon pulls my arm into the air like a winning boxer. I try to pull it down, but she holds it firm.

'She saved my cat!' she yells. 'Roxy rescued Rescue!'

Martin stands on his chair and punches the air. The girls in the class are clapping.

Martin points to Hero. 'You just got done by a girl!' he yells. Then he says to me, 'That was totally Gate One!'

My heart opens like a flower. The room is cheering for me, chanting my name. My name! Like an orchid, I bloom with pride.

Hero has been silent the entire time. It's the quietest he's ever been in a classroom. I slowly turn to meet his glare. If looks could kill, I would be slumped over my desk by now. Bruce and Krew have their heads down.

Hero stands up and slams the desk. 'Stop it!' he shouts.

The class silences.

No one's noticed Sergeant Major standing in the doorway, beetle-browed, arms crossed, playing his elbows like a harp. No one also knows how long he has been there, but I suspect a while.

Sergeant Major walks over to the laptop and presses Stop.

'Geography,' he announces, as if nothing happened.

I reach over and squeeze Cinnamon's hand. I make a heart with my thumbs and index fingers.

She holds up one finger. 'Gate One,' she whispers. 'We're getting there!'

'I can't go on!' Cinnamon screams.

I brace the rope across my stomach with my left hand and brake the extension behind my back with my right. Cinnamon is stranded on the climbing wall, its coloured rocks a jigsaw puzzle she can't work out.

'You can't fall, Cim. You're only a ruler's length off the ground!' I say.

'I'm going to die. I can't do this, let me down,' she squeals.

'Remember flying? Gate Three? This isn't as high as that!'

Everyone in the rock-climbing centre is looking at us now. Sergeant Major has divided us up into pairs and kids are crawling all over the walls like ants. Some are taking on the five-metre-high wall, but Cinnamon and I are still on the beginners wall.

'That was different, no one was watching, you were holding me,' she says, quivering.

I begin to loosen the rope, but a strong hand stops me. 'No,' Sergeant Major commands. He turns to Cinnamon, who is dangling against the wall. One foot is thrust into a green hold large enough to be a shoebox, and both hands are gripping holds that have finger grooves in them to make it easier. 'Climb, girl!' he says. 'You can do this.'

Cinnamon begins to shake. The harness is digging into her legs and I worry it is cutting off her circulation.

'Don't break the wall!' Hero yells. He is hanging upside down on the wall, more than five metres in the air. Even from that distance, his nastiness rots the atmosphere, making Cinnamon's harness rattle even more with nervousness. She braves letting go with her right hand to pull her T-shirt down over her exposed bellybutton.

I tighten my grip, feeling nervous too. I weigh a lot less than Cinnamon and if she falls, even thirty centimetres, I will hurtle towards the ceiling.

'Climb, Cinnamon!' Sergeant Major commands again.

'I can't, I can't, I can't,' Cinnamon squeals.

'C'mon, Cim,' I call. 'You can do it. You're stronger than you know.'

Cinnamon shakes her head violently. She was strong when we were flying, but she's turned all marshmallow: gooey in the centre and scalded on the outside by Hero's taunts.

'Listen to Roxy,' Sergeant Major says. He points to a hold above Cinnamon's head. 'Reach for it, Cinnamon,' he orders.

'Just like you're reaching for cake!' Hero yells.

Sergeant Major strides towards Hero and in eight steps is at the bottom of the wall. He is the only man in the world who could still look deadly in rock-climbing slippers.

'Be quiet, or next time I won't tell you so nicely,' Sergeant Major calls up to him. Then he returns to Cinnamon and steps up to the wall to talk quietly to her. 'Everyone else is climbing the five-metre wall. You need to advance to that in order to pass Phys Ed. Roxy, give her some slack,' he tells me. 'Now reach, Cinnamon.'

Cinnamon takes one finger off the wall, then freezes again. Her hair twitches with tension.

'That's it, bring her down,' he tells me.

Cinnamon still doesn't move. He reaches up, grabs her by the waist and gently lifts her down. As soon as her feet touch the ground, she wraps her arms around me.

Ms Broadfoot, the PE teacher, has brought Year Ten to the rock-climbing centre as well. I look over to where Elecktra and Jackson are spotting each other on the five-metre wall. Lecky is wearing hot-pink bike shorts underneath her school netball skirt. She's bouncing on the wall and giggling. Jackson seems mesmerised by her. My heart aches. His strong forearms bulge as he supports her weight. I can't take my eyes off those arms.

Once Elecktra's back on the ground, she swaggers over to me. 'Jackson said I floated down like an angel,' she says.

'Liar,' I say.

'You're just jealous,' she says.

I roll my eyes and walk away, but Elecktra follows.

Cinnamon is nibbling a biscuit from her lunchbox to calm herself after the climbing ordeal. Crumbs powder her chin.

'Don't worry,' Elecktra says to her. 'I'm not judging you.'

Cinnamon stops chewing. She swallows hard, and is saved by Brandice Spark.

'Ohmigod!' Brandice squeals at Elecktra. 'I love your style so much, I'm going to invent a "love" button for Facebook coz those bike shorts are an update.'

Elecktra dips her hip. 'At least someone appreciates me,' she says, then turns and walks back to the wall.

I glare at Brandice Spark. She has to be the most annoying girl in the world, but at least she took the heat off my friend.

Sergeant Major then takes over as my spotter and sends me up the five-metre wall. Jackson and I have been training intensively in the dojang all week: first harnessing the Tiger Scroll of Water (invisibility), then Fire (weaponry) and Wind (flying). I race easily up and down the five-metre wall. Being undercover ninja has its advantages.

Sergeant Major orders Hero and me to advance to the ten-metre wall. We are the only kids in Year Seven to get this far.

'If you can scale that wall,' he tells us, 'you'll get an A plus for PE.'

I've never got an A plus in anything. Sergeant Major checks our harnesses, then gathers everyone around to watch and learn.

'You belay Roxy first,' Sergeant Major orders Hero.

Hero's eyes are full of black mischief. He grins nastily, running the rope through his hands like an umbilical cord he's about to bite off with fangs. My legs go weak.

'He's going to kill you,' Cinnamon whispers.

I don't reply, terrified she will hear the tremor in my voice.

Jackson makes the wind sign at me, crossing his hands at his chest then bringing them down to his sides. Elecktra is next to him. She looks at me and slips her hand into his. He removes his, but still can't help staring at her as if she's a work of art. I feel sick in my stomach. Even if I can climb this wall like a monkey, he'll never look at me like that. I'm just a Year Seven, Gate Two girl.

'You think about what happened the other night?' Hero asks as I step up onto the first hold. 'You better stop hunting the White Warrior.'

'I've made up my mind,' I say.

I feel the rope tighten around my hips. Out of the corner of my eye, I see him snarl. The kids surrounding us are silent. Even Sergeant Major seems to be holding his breath, keeping a close eye on everything. My fingertips are slippery with sweat. I don't trust Hero, and now he has my life in his hands. I feel like Rescue, hovering over the toilet, about to be plunged to his death.

I reach for two holds above my head so my body is flat against the wall. I close my eyes and let the spectators' expectations blow through me. I feel the air rise and collapse my lungs, the pores of my skin expand and contract, I become aware of every particle of air within me and around me. Just as Jackson taught me, I find the sliver of breath connected to the world like a silver wire and fasten myself to it. I allow that wire of breath to propel me up and away.

I leap up towards another hold, projecting all four points of my body off the wall at once. I land crouched on a single hold. The crowd gasps. I fling my body up higher and land on one foot, almost balancing on my big toe.

I look down and see Jackson still gazing at Elecktra. I no longer feel nausea in the pit of my stomach, but fire. I propel higher to reach the ten-metre mark and the class claps. I wait on the hold for a few seconds, taking in the applause.

I find a sliver of air and propel myself forwards again. The class cheers. The rope is slack, giving me freedom. I look down and Hero isn't watching me as he should be, he's talking to Krew and pointing at something. I see the power in his body as he leans into the harness and supports my weight. I am only two metres now from the top of the wall. I take a deep breath and launch myself off the wall, aiming for the very highest hold.

As my body glides through the air, I feel my harness tighten around my hips. Then I'm detaching from that sliver of air and the wire that was pulling me up becomes slack, the wind beneath me flattens and I begin to fall. My harness is yanked violently and I'm not just falling, I'm plummeting. I scream. The rope tightens and jolts me just before I smash to the ground. A glass-shattering pain fires up my arm and into my shoulder, sharper than a sword.

Hero's lips are at my ear. 'You'll never be Gate One,' he says. 'And thanks for the Tiger Scrolls.'

Then pain engulfs me and the world switches to dark.

EIGHTEEN

I wake squinting into the fluorescent light, blinking myself into the foreign surroundings. I'm in a hospital bed. The room smells of bleach. Art is asleep next to me in an armchair, quietly snoring. I look down at my arm in a plaster cast and taste metal in my mouth. 'Art,' I call.

Art jerks awake and lunges to my side. 'How you feeling?' he asks, pressing his hand to my forehead. 'You broke your arm in that climbing class and passed out from the pain.' He rearranges the blankets around me.

'I'm such a wimp,' I say and Art laughs. But the smile dies quickly from my lips as I remember the Tiger Scrolls. 'My school bag!' I yelp, trying to push myself up.

Art stops me and lifts the school bag off the ground. I grab the bottom with my good arm and turn it upside down, shaking out its contents; books, pens, lunchbox and a few adzuki beans rattle onto the bed, but no Tiger Scrolls. I burst into tears.

'It's okay,' Art soothes. 'I'm sure you don't need to worry about your homework for a while.'

'I'm not worried about my homework,' I sob. Hero must have had Krew steal the scrolls out of my bag while I was climbing. I can't believe I didn't see that coming. The tears rain down my cheeks, then splash onto my cast. A nurse comes in, but Art waves 'it's okay'. He moves my arm away from the fountain of tears.

'Look, Cat, I know it's hard with Mum being away. I know you wish she was here now, instead of me.' He wraps an arm around me. 'But I'll look after you. We'll cook marshmallows in the living-room fire?' he offers.

I smile at him thinly and blow my nose on the tissue he offers me. I can't tell him about the Tiger Scrolls. 'Sounds great,' I say bleakly.

Falling off the climbing wall in front of the class is hitting social rock bottom, because when I go back to school, everyone is acting totally weird. No one is looking at me and no one is talking to me. When I was in hospital, Cinnamon and Jackson didn't even call to see if I was okay.

I have to find Jackson to talk about training. There's no way I can go through with this White Warrior hunt. Hero can keep the scrolls. I'll go back to being a lame Year Seven, Gate Twoer, and Elecktra can defend herself against Hero if he ever visits again. She can bore him to death with her acting.

'Cinnamon,' I call, running up to her.

She turns her head away. 'I can't speak to you,' she whispers.

'Why not?'

'I can't say.'

'My arm's okay, by the way,' I say, lifting my sling towards her.

Jackson approaches. 'My god, Roxy, I didn't know the fall was so serious,' he blurts, pointing to my cast.

Jackson envelops me in a bear hug. His washing powder mixed with home-made pasta sauce scent juices into the space between us. When he releases me, I realise his school blazer has a hole cut out of it in the shape of a heart. His light-blue school shirt beams through. I point to it with my good hand.

'Elecktra,' he sighs. 'She didn't take it well.'

My eyes widen.

'I told her I don't think we're soul mates,' he finishes.

My heart flutters, eclipsing the pain in my arm. He smiles at me and I feel all shiny new again.

He spots Elecktra down the hall, fanning herself with *Vogue* magazine beside her locker. Her school tie is wrapped around her head like a headband, her golden locks cascading down her shoulders like silk. Kids stare at her as they traipse down the hall; just the sight of her makes you feel inadequate.

Jackson storms towards her. The crowd parts, then closes in around them.

Elecktra flicks me off, then spears her dark river eyes towards Jackson.

'You're mad!' he says.

'I'd rather be mad than,' Elecktra pauses for dramatic effect, 'heartless,' she says, pointing to his heart cut-out and laughing. 'You're lucky I didn't do more damage!'

They've only been dating in her mind and she's already broken up with him.

Jackson clenches his fists in frustration. I'm used to her not making sense, but it infuriates other people when they don't speak 'Elecktrafied'.

I'm about to ask Cinnamon what's going on when a hand the size of a baseball mitt lands on my backpack. I wince as my injured arm gets knocked.

'Looking for you,' Sergeant Major says.

He leads me down the corridor in front of all the kids. I don't know what hurts more, my arm or the humiliation. He dumps me in the staff room, which stinks. All the teachers look furious when they see me. Many of them are holding handkerchiefs to their faces. Our science teacher, Dr Klemky, is wearing a snorkelling mask that he uses to protect his nose during extreme experiments, and the school nurse has a surgical mask over her nose and mouth. The room smells of burning and something disgusting, like old compost. I notice a gaping black hole in the carpet and my stomach cramps.

Principal Cheatley steps forwards, his hand over his nose. 'Roxy Ran, you're suspended,' he says.

I look at the teachers, bewildered. They glare back at me.

'Why?' I say.

'Why?' Sergeant Major yells. 'We thought the school was burning down! There were seven or so fires in here. I extinguished them by stomping on them in my new boots,' he booms.

'We all came running and started stomping,' Principal Cheatley cuts in. 'Dr Klemky, Ms Broadfoot, myself — all of us stomping out these fires.'

'And that's when we found your presents!' Sergeant Major yells.

The sun is streaming through the window and heating up the burned patches of carpet. The smell is unbearable, rancid, like off meat.

'What presents?' I blurt, not having a clue.

'The brown paper bags of fertiliser you set on fire!' Sergeant Major yells.

'I didn't,' I stutter.

'Don't try to get out of it — we found this on the floor.' He holds out my notebook with the list of things that make me feel good. 'And there was a witness. The groundskeeper said he saw you.'

'I didn't do it! It's a set-up! I've been in hospital!' I say frantically, holding up my sling as proof. 'Someone must have stolen —'

Sergeant Major puts his hand up in my face. 'Silence,' he commands.

'You're suspended for four days,' Principal Cheatley says. 'We've phoned your mother's partner, he's on his way.'

I cast my eyes down at Sergeant Major's boots: they are singed black. He's never going to forgive me. Ms Broadfoot's runners are black too — there goes my A plus in PE.

'But I didn't do it,' I say again.

Principal Cheatley glares at me. 'The school could have burned down, staff and pupils could have been injured, and it's going to cost a fortune to replace the carpet. And where are the teachers meant to eat lunch? The playground?' His face swells with rage.

There is no point trying to speak. The old Roxy is in the room and, as good as I've got at fighting, I can never fight her.

* * *

'Hey.' Jackson taps me on the shoulder as I gather my things from my locker.

I turn to him, my good arm full of books. His eyes are green jungles of light and shade.

'Got suspended, thanks to Hero's fertiliser bombs. He must have told Krew to steal my notebook out of my school bag when he stole the Tiger Scrolls,' I say.

'Hero's got the scrolls!' Jackson's eyes explode. He grips his head.

I shrug. 'Jackson, I give up. I'm retiring.'

'Hero's furious over the video,' Jackson says, scratching his chest through the heart. He then pushes his hand through his hair to the back of his neck, leaning his head against his arm. No doubt out of all his moves, this is his best.

'I could do with a holiday from school anyway,' I say.

Suddenly, Jackson's face drains of colour.

I drop my books in fright. 'What's wrong?'

'I don't want to freak you out,' he says.

'What? What is it?' I say.

'It's happening. They're calling you.'

'Who?'

'The ancient warriors. The mark of the warrior is on your forehead.' He points.

I turn to the mirror on my locker door. There are three black stripes appearing across my forehead like fresh scars. I can't breathe. I feel like Jackson's got my neck in a pressure hold. I'm not ready. I don't even know that I want to do this.

I manage to croak, 'What does this mean? How long have I got?'

'A couple of hours,' he says and takes my hand. I can't tell if I'm shaking because of that or because I'm terrified.

'Hey, a life without a bit of adventure is boring,' he says, then adds, 'I only wish that I could be there, fighting with you.'

I look away, watching the corridor fill with kids, all oblivious that we live in a world of ninja magic and samurai threat. If I don't find the White Warrior, all this will change forever. The world will be divided into those who protect and those who kill.

'I believe in you.' Jackson squeezes my hand. 'Do you believe in you?'

'How am I meant to fight with a broken arm? I'll be toast in a second,' I say, trying not to tremble.

Jackson smiles mysteriously. 'Your arm will be okay,' he says. 'Trust me.'

I do trust Jackson, but time is running out.

'I have to get my ninja on,' I say.

NINETEEN

Wearing my ninja uniform is like a superhero moment that helps me transform into character. In your uniform, it doesn't matter who you've been in the past; your *shinobi shozoku* reminds you that you can be anything you want. Dressing in my uniform is the most important part of preparing for the fight. As soon as the material touches my body, I feel like I become someone else, a performer taking the stage or a sprinter on their marks.

I carefully thread my broken arm through my ninja jacket. My ninja jacket has no ties or tails and makes me feel slick and fast. I fold the hood over my hair. The hood covers my mouth so I can hear my breath at all times; a link to my heart. A fierce wind blasts through the window and blows my black hair out of the hood and across my forehead, flapping against the black warrior stripes. My eyes glimmer with ferocious energy, tigerish brown beneath the black scars.

In my black uniform, against the stark light of my bedroom lamp, I no longer look lame or feel invisible. I look like me, Roxy Ran, thirteen years old and lethal. All those times I allowed Elecktra to dress me up in silly outfits, I never had the guts to say I felt uncomfortable. But now, looking at myself in my ninja suit, I realise that I don't need Elecktra to accept me; all this time I needed to accept myself.

'I am ninja,' I say to the mirror.

I no longer see the awkward kid who gets spat on at school or ditched by her own sister. I see someone fierce, feminine — a fighter. I jump into a strong horse-riding stance, with my hands in fists on my hips, surprised that my broken arm doesn't hurt as much. I see someone with legs that could break rocks. I perform ten whipping punches to the mirror, then bend my knees lower and jump to clap my heels together in the air. I land in the same strong stance.

'As a ninja, my body is a weapon, my movements are magical, my focus is lethal. I am the invisible warrior,' I recite.

The words from the ancient ninja's Tiger Scrolls charge my cells with power. Nerve by nerve I feel the force surge through me and soon I'm bolstered with confidence.

'Those warriors better watch out,' I say to the mirror.

I pack my weapons. I fit the horn rings on my fingers, tuck the nunchucks in my belt, and sling the bow and arrows over my shoulder with the *katana* sword. In my ninja utility belt I organise my ninja stars, firebombs, birds' eggs, chain and sickle, blowpipe and poisonous paper darts. I pause to think of Jackson: teaching me how to make a bamboo bow, climb the dojang walls, make firebombs. I wish he was with me, but this is something I have to do alone.

I start tying my two-toed *tabi*. If I think too much, I could chicken out. I recall Jackson's words: *You don't have to learn; you only have to remember. It's in your blood. Instinct.* The tiger roars within me and I feel the clawing of excitement in my heart. Fire simmers in my bones, a burning power and strength that will explode unless unleashed.

I stand at the window and close my eyes. I am ready. The fire burns stronger. I realise now that it comes from my birthmark, which beats and roars with the heart of a tiger. A source of power I am only just learning to harness, and that will transport me to the Cemetery of Warriors.

I allow the fire I've been struggling to contain all these weeks to spread, from my heart out to the tips of my fingers. When every cell is alight and I am completely consumed, I flicker three times, then disappear.

* * *

I have never experienced complete darkness before. It feels as if all air and brightness have been crushed.

Then the darkness parts and green moonlight diffuses through a black leathery mist. Fog wreaths around my ankles, and in the distance I can just make out a hill. Uncertain at first, then drawing confidence from my inner tiger, I run towards it. As I climb, there is a deathly silence. All I can hear is my own panting. As I'm running, I feel my cast loosen. A flood of relief rushes into my bones. I hear a crack and look down — my cast has broken off. And Jackson knew all along my arm would heal here. The smell of rancid meat wafts from below and in the green moonlight I see a vast graveyard on the other side of the hill, with derelict tombs, vaults, gravestones and crypts. In their centre is a cleared circle filled with shimmering blue smoke.

'The Circle of Self-defence,' I whisper.

Jackson told me about this circle, where dark and light meet to create a blue disc that illuminates all combat within its merciless surrounds. Once I enter the circle, I must fight.

I have the feeling of being watched. I look around to see thousands of ancient warriors standing next to their tombs, waiting for the entertainment: another intruder attempting to find the White Warrior. I suppress a gasp of horror as I realise they are each armed and ready to attack me.

I approach the circle. A brutal wind blasts across the graveyard and scatters the fog. My panting is louder and faster in the silence. I think of my mother, remember being strapped to her back as she battled the samurai. Now it is my turn to fight. I step into the circle.

Suddenly, the sky scours red; not a warm red like a crackling log fire, but the blistering red of an infected cut. Smoke swirls around me. I bow my head as Jackson taught me and wait.

I hear footsteps and my heart seizes. They are thunderous, cracking the earth's crust and tearing the air apart. My mouth turns dirt dry, my hands sweat, but I do not flinch. Then a putrid smell hits me, snapping my attention upwards. There is a hand in the darkness, and it holds a sword.

Hanzo glares down at me. He is four metres tall. His *shinobi shozoku* fits him like a black snakeskin so you can't distinguish between it and his own flesh. A metal muzzle covers his nose and mouth, and his eyes are two glowing white-bone sockets. Jackson was right. He is the grossest thing I've ever seen. My heart beats as my knees turn to water.

He holds the sword out at shoulder height above me. It is made of gold with a gleaming black bone handle. As the smoke waves past it, the blade sparks, a deadly razor. If it sliced you, you wouldn't even know you'd been cut. Your limb would fall off so cleanly, you'd be watching it roll away before the pain came crashing in. I swallow hard.

Hanzo points the sword to the sky and its tip disappears into the gaping wound. There is a clap of thunder and the sword explodes into a pillar of flames. Hanzo's white, soulless eyes glow brighter and the muzzle lifts as his mouth twists into a crooked smile. He levels the sword at shoulder height again, but now there is a gleaming apple stuck on its burning tip. The world blacks out. All that exists is the flaming sword. I jump as a length of material sweeps across my eyes. A blindfold. Now I am left with only four senses.

I hear the old Roxy in my head. 'You can't do it, you'll fail.' Her voice is a grater against my heart. I try to take the blindfold off, but it is fastened to my temples. I stand motionless. I'm blind, so I can't run. I don't know how to transport back home. There's nowhere to hide and no one to save me.

No one except myself.

I raise my hands into a fighting guard, crunch my fingers into fists and spike out my horn rings. I stand strong, and slowly the panic washes away. I can smell Hanzo. In the blackness, his putrefying vapour, a blend of rotting cheese and the fetid odour of burning flesh, forms a map of movement. I search the labyrinth of my memory and have a flash of an apple splitting open like a firework, bitten by the teeth of a tiger. I take a step backwards, lick my lips and focus my body.

'Don't miss,' the old Roxy warns me.

'Be quiet!' I yell.

I feel my heart ripping open like the sky, the nerves in my body tense, the oxygen in my blood thrusting.

'My focus is lethal,' I whisper to myself.

I feel blazing sparks from the sword above me showering onto my ninja hood. I push the old Roxy away and call on my inner warrior. I bend my knees, load my ankles with weight, then shoot my body into the air. I catapult upwards, feeling the air split across my blindfold. When my inner warrior yells, 'Three!', I spin three times, extending my leg out behind me and hooking my toes into the apple like teeth, chopping it into several pieces. My blindfold dissolves as I fall back to earth and land, crouching, where I started. To my disbelief, the apple falls around me like glittering emerald rain.

When I look up, Hanzo has disappeared.

I did it!

The fog folds around me and interrupts my sense of victory. I am alone, yet the intense feeling of being watched continues. I shudder, remembering all those dead warriors in the graveyard. Then I think of saving Rescue in the boys' toilets and the exhilaration of my first fight. My tiger roars again. I'm here, at what could be my last fight, and I am no longer fighting bullies, but monsters.

There is no time to rest. There is a rush of wind, like a tornado, and a sound like helicopter blades overhead. When I look up, I am blinded by blue smoke. Bright swathes of orange fabric appear out of the haze, in their centre a spinning body. The fabric blades are vast enough to be two burnished skies; they sizzle against the red backdrop of the night. Old Roxy's voice slithers in my ear. 'Second time not so lucky.' I suddenly want Jackson, Mum, Elecktra, all of them here to hold my hand, to cheer me on. I am completely alone.

The orange blades fall suddenly flat. The eruption of silence bursts my eardrums. I double over and scream as the pain knifes into my brain. Then the ringing stops and I'm able to stumble to my feet.

The Shaolin Monk cranes up from his robes into a fighting stance. His eyes are milky blue with cataracts. He is thousands of years dead, the original master of

Kung Fu. When he lowers his chin, his bald skull snarls open into a deep mouth with fanged teeth.

I feel the teeth of the tiger on my sole growl. I snap out of my scared state and feel a wave of adrenalin punch through me. I summon my physical combat skills, building the blocks of kicks, strikes, holds, flips, pressure points into a fortress of defence. This will be a brutal fight.

'I'm not sure you're up for it,' old Roxy says.

I ignore her and wait, listening to the sound of my own breathing, the sound of my own mortality.

I hear a distant chiming of cymbals and the Shaolin Monk begins scorpion boxing, snaking across the floor, stinging me with his feet. His technique is beautiful and I can't help but admire the speed of his strikes.

The Monk's percussive hand strikes fly at me and I meet them with my horn rings, nunchucks and tiger heel. Somehow, I know to match his scorpion boxing with leopard boxing. I can't help feeling proud that I've remembered my training and that it works, even in another realm!

The Monk crouches with his arms spread above him like a crane. I pause in tiger stance, waiting. Perhaps to him I look like a well-trained ninja, but beneath my uniform I feel like a terrified young girl. I'm on the verge of tears and grateful that my *shinobi shozoku* covers my mouth so he can't see my lips trembling. I cross my arms across my chest in an effort to stop my hands shaking.

In the distance a drum begins to beat. The circle clears of smoke. The Monk's head snarls. The skin across my chest stretches as tight as that drum and, with every beat, I feel more and more fear.

The Monk charges at me. He backflips, tucks his knees under his chin, touches the ground once and spins twice to land into a forward roll so fast that he sparks fire. When he stands, he has a staff in his hand.

I gulp and instinctively raise my arms above my head and tense my stomach. The Monk swings the staff back behind his neck, then gallops forwards and smashes it across my stomach. The blow thunders through me, rattling my bones, but I won't allow it to shatter my spirit. All my training culminates in this moment, when I'm standing against a master of technique.

'My movements are magical,' I say aloud. I will not be defeated by him. I take a deep breath, centre my spirit and brace for the fight.

We engage in hand-to-hand combat, percussive strikes met by inner and outside blocks. I leap and land my elbow in the centre of the Monk's back. He pushes me away with both hands, followed by a flying side kick that sends me to the ground so hard my body grooves out a channel of earth. I stand instantly, sweep kick his ankles, but he jumps over my feet and retaliates with a spinning crescent kick into my ear.

The blue smoke rises around us like waves, the circle awash with turbulence that reflects the feelings inside me. I don't know if I have the strength to continue. My skin is bruised and swollen, my bones ache. But then I think of my mother, her ninja stars slicing the air, the strike of her dagger, and no matter the pain, nothing will be more painful than failing her, failing to reach for the stars. I remember my hard-boiled egg and my mother's word: fortitude. Now I understand.

The Monk charges at me again and I wait, heart in mouth, then smash a double back fist into his torso. His hands fall on my shoulders in blades. I catch one of them, twist it behind his back and punch him forwards with my leg. He lands on his face, but jumps up a second later without using his hands. It didn't work. Again, tears threaten.

The Monk hits me with a triple roundhouse kick, one in my shins, one in my stomach and, finally, a snipe to the face. I feel my jaw dislocate, but have no time for pain. I turn into his kicks, bend down to grab him at the knees and use his force against him to flip his body over my head. I stare in disbelief. My training works.

I can tell by her silence that even old Roxy is impressed.

'That's what you get for being so ancient,' I say to the Monk.

He lies motionless. Blue smoke smears across his body and I see the shadow of orange radiating behind it. In a blink, he evaporates into pink steam.

Instead of celebrating, I bow into my starting position again and concentrate on my breathing. I think of training with Jackson, and the memory of his moss-green eyes cools my burning skin and aching bones. I turn my neck to the side, grab my chin and forehead between my hands to crack my jaw back into place, but realise it has already healed. I'd forgotten that in the Cemetery of Warriors wounds heal magically. I thank my inner warrior for the strength to go on.

TWENTY

Gusts of wind serrate the surfaces of the graves around me. The blue air glitters as if a giant hand was scattering gold ashes. Fresh air streams into the circle, and when I look up I see an ash-grey silhouette on the other side of the vast blue expanse. It gives off a vanilla scent, like orchids — the smell of the living. When a mass of blonde hair explodes out of the hood and spirals in the wind, I know I am no longer alone in the world of the dead.

'Mum!'

I want to run to her, but she yells, 'Stay!'

I stop, and hear more footsteps, earth-clashing and speeding towards the circle. It sounds like they're coming from every direction; an army of warriors racing towards us.

Mum and I look upwards as a great battle cry splits the sky, causing it to bleed again. When I look back down, I see the Apache Warrior powering towards me, his tomahawk in the air. His hair is alive, thick black eels lashing against his back; his eyes are hollow and his face is threaded with dark wide scars. He is bare-chested and barefooted. Every step he takes sparks fireballs in the blue mist, which spew forth showers of burning stars. He is running so fast I am stripped of my fear and of my reflexes; his battle cry swamps my thinking. His tomahawk isn't pointed at me, but at Mum.

'No!' I yell.

'Water!' Mum screams.

I remember the orchid sign on my mother's ninja star, and the meaning of my name. Then it comes. 'I am the invisible warrior,' I say. I close my eyes, using darkness to extinguish the flames of fear. I force myself to breathe in the heat of the warrior, to consume his power. I summon the tiger's power from within. When my spirit is centred, I open my eyes, just in time to see the Apache's tomahawk fly from his hand towards my mother's throat. I flash invisible and catch the tomahawk a hair's width from her neck. Mum's eyes are fastened shut. I spear the tomahawk towards the sky and into the wound caused by the warrior's battle cry.

The Apache Warrior stops in his tracks and bows towards me. When he lifts his head, I see a knowing glimmer in his eyes, a hint of a smirk, a shadow of evil before he vanishes. And then I hear it. The grating of knives.

I turn to Mum and reach out to hug her. 'Whatever you do, don't —' Her eyes flinch pain and, just as I grasp her shoulders, she fades away, her sentence unfinished.

I am left alone to face the final warrior.

My heart ticks like a bomb; my attempts to make sense of what I'm hearing are too slow, knuckle-dragging. 'Whatever you do' repeats over and over in my head. Don't do what? How did Mum even know I was here? I begin to tremble. The sound of grating knives calls back every one of Hero's taunts — they fly at me like daggers.

'Hero's right,' old Roxy says. 'You're pathetic.'

I shake the old Roxy off, then feel a hot breath on my neck. I turn and standing behind me is a mountainous Gladiator. His face is shrouded by a silver mask and his helmet is adorned with cascading ropes of blazing red feathers. The helmet extends into a single sleeve of armour down his left arm, but where his hand should be there is a ball and chain. He is wearing a leather vest over chainmail, and shields over his shins that extend to mid-thigh. Racks of knives are draped across his chest and he is scraping them with his axe. His eyes are white bone, shining through the mask. What little I can see of his face is a mess of pus and decay. He's hideous.

In his right hand he carries a bow and arrows. I think of my poor bow and arrow skills.

'You're finished,' old Roxy says.

The Gladiator's weapons are stained with old blood. He is over two metres tall, with muscles that writhe like wild beasts trapped in a net of skin. He sucks the wind into his mouth, then bellows at me with the power of all the elements. I block the blast with my hands; my skin feels as if it's stripping from my bones. My cheeks blow back to my ears, my hood blasts off my head, my hair tugs at its roots. My teeth chatter, but I hold myself strong. This is my final test. I've come too far to give in now. I take a slow step forwards into the monster's filthy breath.

The Gladiator winds up his ball and chain and smashes it to the ground. The earth shudders. A canyon opens up, forcing me to leap across the circle. He slams his ball and chain into the earth again and the Circle of Self-defence splits in half. If his ball can split the circle, imagine what it will do to my arms and legs!

He strikes his ball and chain into the ground again and again, transforming the cemetery into a cratered battlefield. He ploughs the graves with his fierce weapon and moves towards me. All around us, skulls and bones are unearthed, but there is not a soul to be seen.

I move into a long stance with my hands above my head in a knife-hand upper block, trying to disguise my trembling fingers. I run through my weapons in my head and suddenly remember my ninja star with the orchid sign. It is small enough to grasp without the Gladiator noticing, and its blades will enmesh in that chain if I can spin it accurately.

'Come back to me,' I whisper to my boomerang star.

I wait for the Gladiator to whip the ball into the air again, then, as if in slow motion, the blue haze slows the weapon midair. I have just enough time to flick the star out of my wrist and send it flying towards the chain. The star veers to the left, past the Gladiator, slicing into his armoured sleeve but barely denting it. It boomerangs back to my hand and I catch it with a thud of horror.

The Gladiator raises his bow and aims it at me. He pulls back his powerful elbow, then releases the arrows. I watch them spinning towards me and my heart stops. I'm paralysed with fear. And then I hear my soul whispering to me: 'My body is a weapon.'

I leap as high as I can, backflip above the Gladiator's head and land on his shoulders. He thrashes to throw me off. The arrows spear off into the distance. I grab the feathers on his helmet and, as his ball and chain lashes into the air, I jump onto the ball and kick it into his helmet. It catches there, and as the ball plummets to the ground the Gladiator's head is yanked down with it ... and rolls off into the distance. And still he comes.

When his head smashes against the ground, I pull out my nunchucks and begin working them over my shoulder in a figure-eight motion. When the Gladiator's arm reaches towards me, I slice off his hand with a single whip of my chains. But even with no head and only one hand, he continues towards me.

I draw my sword. I spin three times, lunge into a back stance, then plough forwards into cat stance, sitting deep and low, aiming my sword at his heart. I think of my mother. She fought with me strapped to her back; now I must fight with her strapped to my heart. I know that if I spear the Gladiator and he falls, I will be crushed. I plant the handle of the sword in the earth so its blade points upwards, then, just before the Gladiator reaches me, I catapult into the air into a double side splits.

The Gladiator lands on my sword. I see the tip of my blade appear through the leather of his back armour. Blue smoke clouds over the Gladiator and he disappears. My feet are once again stable on the ground.

I look around, expecting to see the White Warrior revealed. Nothing. Maybe I have to fight more monsters. The thought is terrifying and I feel tears prickling my eyes. Despite beating all four warriors, I feel defeated.

I stab the tears away with my thumbs. 'Be strong, Roxy,' I tell myself. I dart my eyes left and right, but there is no sign of the White Warrior with the mark on his soul. No sign of the Tiger Scrolls. How do I get home?

TWENTY-ONE

When the smoke clears, a figure emerges, only a little taller than me. When it steps into the green light of the moon, my heart stops.

'Hero?' I whisper to myself.

The sight of him sends needles down my spine. Fear clutches my heart with burning talons. I clench my teeth to stop them from chattering. It is easier to fight the unknown than the known.

Hero is dressed in his traditional red samurai kimono with *katana* swords strapped to his back. In his hands he holds the ancient ninja's Tiger Scrolls.

'You're not the only one training to find the White Warrior,' he reminds me.

He walks to the edge of the Circle of Self-defence and places the Tiger Scrolls at the base of an alabaster tombstone. The leather book looks more worn and delicate. This is what the White Warrior wants. Now he might appear.

Hero wastes no time. He steps into the circle, and light wisps from him and blurs into the smoke. Before I can move, his heel hits me in the stomach. I double over. All I can see is a mash of green and purple spots. The first blow always stings.

He pulls me upright and twists my arm behind my back. 'Transport home. You're done,' he croons in my ear.

For a nanosecond, the tears bubble. I don't know how to get home. What if I'm stuck here among the dead forever?

He wrings my arm like a towel and I clench my teeth against the pain. I am limp in his grip for a moment, thinking. I've spent my life allowing people like Hero to put me down, to rule me. It's time to stand up for myself. No more feeling invisible for the wrong reasons.

'No,' I say and kick my foot straight up past my shoulder, into his face behind me. 'Meet my pet tiger!' I yell.

Hero falls backwards, cupping his nose. 'That mark on your sole,' he says, stumbling.

I say nothing, watching his fingertips, his hips, his ankles for any sign of his next move.

He walks up to me. I brace for another attack. His eyes simmer with hatred. Blue smoke swirls around us and the smell of the dead reminds me of what lies ahead if we are too slow or too weak. Despite the stench, I take a deep breath, knowing it could be my last chance to take in the oxygen needed to fight.

'It's always been you,' he says.

I don't understand. But before I can think further, Hero launches his attack. Body punches and upper cuts stab me in the chest and the ribs. I duck and weave, punching him away. I'm not used to feeling human bone crunch under my knuckles and am not sure I like it.

When I tear my fist from his shoulder, the cloth of his kimono tears away with it. He looks down at the rip, registering my strength, then looks back up at me with his eyes smiling evil.

He punches me again and I catch his arm, snap his outer elbow with a knife-hand strike. His arm bends backwards and dangles helplessly. He winces, then cracks it back into position and assumes a long stance upper block, swivelling his back foot around to follow me as I move in and out of range, trying to anticipate his next move. His eyes shadow my injuries; I can taste blood running from my nose and feel swelling in my eyes. I've banished old Roxy; she sits on a nearby tomb, watching silently as ninja Roxy takes the stage.

I move in to strike, but I'm too slow and my cheek meets Hero's spinning hook kick. I feel my jaw jar again and my teeth realign, but the fire within forces me upright and into a spinning double back kick. The kick ploughs into Hero's chest, crashing him to the outer edge of the circle. He lands on his feet and draws his sword from his back, then charges at me.

Before I can blink, the blade is at my throat. I have just enough time to push his wrist away with one arm and gouge his eyes with my other hand.

'Tell me why you hate me so much,' I say.

Before he can answer, the earth shatters between us and breaks us apart. I knew the ancient warriors would still be testing me!

The ground rises into a skyscraper of dirt that soars towards the green heavens, and we are stranded on a small circular platform with a sheer drop in every direction. Up here, the air is thin and I have trouble breathing. The sky is a burnished copper flecked with jaundiced clouds that are beaten by wind and thunder. Our fighting arena looks like a hovering blue disc of smoke, its haze streaming over the edges and pooling down below. If we don't stay within its perimeter, we will fall to our deaths.

Far below, the tombstone where Hero placed the Tiger Scrolls glows alabaster in the shadows, a beacon. I have to get those scrolls!

I turn around, but Hero is closer than I'd anticipated and I spin straight into his grip. He strangles my throat.

I try to beat him away, but he doesn't flinch. My tongue swells and I feel the veins choke in my forehead.

'Go!' I say to myself, then jump knee him in the groin and scurry backwards as far as the platform will allow, heaving in air. Tears come again and I can't help it. It feels as though he has already hurt me more than the ancient warriors did and he's only a kid, like me. I try desperately to form a plan, but I feel too broken to think straight. I have hardly caught my breath when Hero charges at me with a flying hammer fist that strikes me on the side of my neck, choking the air out of me once again.

A second flying hammer fist comes, but this time I block it, roundhouse kick his ear off the front foot, following with a double roundhouse kick to his body, sending him to the centre of the circle. He absorbs the strikes and chases me back towards the edge of the platform. I block him with my legs, my feet fighting to keep him at a distance, biting him with their blades and heels. But Hero moves in close so I can't kick. His knife-hand strikes and chops push me dangerously close to the drop. I stop blocking them to concentrate on not falling off the side, and take the blows to the face. I feel capillaries burst and scabs peel.

Hero steps out and spins twice, then hook kicks, his leg stretching out to the nearest yellow cloud. I pause, mesmerised by the beauty of his technique, then ram his supporting leg like I'm a rugby player. He crumples to the ground, but only for a second before jumping up without using his hands and assuming a crane position. His left eye has swollen, but I see no shiver of pain or weakness.

I leap across the platform and hook punch his cheek. He stands motionless, as though he doesn't feel it, then leans forwards and slaps me across my cheek. My skin burns hot and for a second I am disoriented. The thick buttery clouds blind my sight and I am back in the boys' toilets at school. I remember how strong I felt then, determined to save Rescue; nothing could stand in my way. Those feelings rise within me again and, for the first time, my chest swells with pride.

'You're a bully!' I yell across the circle at Hero.

'I'm samurai!' he yells back.

My vision clears and I kneel into a bow position to centre my mind.

'You'll always be a loser,' he says. 'That's why your father left you.'

Usually his words would stab my heart like serrated knives, but in this moment, as I kneel, aware of my breath entering my body, my chest rising and lowering, my hands relaxed and open on my thighs, the words skim off my shoulders like *shuriken*. I slowly open my eyes. For once, I have control over my feelings. I am able to think positively.

The wind blows the hair not contained by my ninja hood across my eyes. The tower rises higher. Now the clouds are below us. The air thins again, making it even harder to breathe. The ancient warriors are proving their strength. If they can move mountains, I can stay here and fight.

Hero picks up a skull unearthed by the sudden movement of the circle and throws it in the air. He punches it to smithereens, then sinks into a low horse-riding stance.

'Skulls don't hit back,' I say, then pounce on him with triple front kicks between his parted legs. He doubles over, screaming with agony and rage.

I can no longer see the tombstone where the ancient ninja's Tiger Scrolls sit. There is blackness below us and blackness above us. If I can't fight my way out of this, it will be blackness forever.

All I can see is the red of Hero's kimono and the whites of his eyes hungering for my blood. He chases me with kicks. I move backwards, feeling every inch of the platform disappear as I am pushed closer and closer to the edge. I shuffle away from Hero's kicks, but at the cost of losing more ground. The edge looms closer. I dig my feet into the earth with all my strength, but his kicks are too powerful and push me back. He leaps into a double front kick and I know this is it.

I watch his foot fly into my face. His kick flips me backwards and, as I spin, I see the blue disc disappear beneath me. I fall screaming, thrashing my arms and legs in the hope of gripping onto something. I catch the side of the mountain by my fingertips and I hang there for what seems an eternity, gripping the soft earth with my nails and steadying my breathing. Any wrong move and this will be it — I'll never see my family again, never walk through Gate One, never experience my first kiss ...

The fog encases me; I can't see above or below. I clutch the earth blindly. I can't hear Hero. There are tears spilling down my face; I hadn't realised I was crying. My body is numb with pain. All my energy is focused on saving my life.

'You can do this,' I say.

'It's over,' old Roxy says. 'He's whipping you. He's got the scrolls. The White Warrior will appear to him.'

I lean my face into the mud and feel it fill my nostrils. My eyes sting. My forearms are weak. Every part of me is screaming. Maybe old Roxy is right.

'You've always been weak,' she says.

Weak. I lift my face out of the mud. 'I'm not weak,' I say.

Others may think I'm weak, but this is my chance to banish weakness. I hook my feet into a rock below and use the power in my legs to hurl myself up to the next hold, like scaling the climbing wall in Sergeant Major's class. I pause just below the ledge and listen. If I reach my fingers up, Hero will slice them off with his sword. If I lift my head over the ledge to see — there goes my head.

My heart beats against the wall of rock. I decide my head is more precious. I slowly hook my index finger up onto the ledge and I cringe. Nothing. My middle finger joins it. I wince again. Still nothing. I reach my whole hand up, brace … and nothing. I wait, listening. The fog is a thick disguise. Perhaps Hero thinks I plummeted to my death.

When I finally peer over the edge, Hero is nowhere to be seen. I climb onto the disc and dust myself off.

Without warning Hero is flying towards me. I balance on the balls of my feet, then jump in the air, fanning my left arm around in an outside knife-hand block and punching Hero in his chest with my right hand. I land again on the balls of my feet on the outer edge of the platform, and thank my lucky ninja stars for those bamboo-balance lessons. Still balancing on the edge, I punch Hero in his chest as he flies towards me midair, but he punches me at the same time, crunching his knuckles against mine. The impact is enough to send us both out into nothingness, but I manage to propel myself forwards and land on my wrists.

I creep to the centre of the circle, armed with my ninja stars. A great beam reaches up to the clouds, and as it descends I realise it's Hero's leg slicing through the smoke, on its way down to cut me in half. I move out of the way just in time and shin block his axe kick. The power of his kick churns through me, locking my muscles and stiffening my vertebrae.

We break apart and stalk the edge of the platform, the world dropping away beneath us. Hero cracks his neck, opens and closes his hands, rolls his ankles and swipes at the blood dripping from his nose and chin.

I summon all the power and strength within me and recent images speed through my mind: training with Jackson, flying across the rooftops with Cinnamon, the feeling of freedom when I leaped over the toilet wall to save Rescue, learning to be invisible, the first time I held the ninja star, the fear in my mother's eyes before I saved her from the Apache Warrior. The memories combust and my muscles contract, flying me upwards and into a backflip towards Hero so fast he has no time to move. I spring onto his shoulders and assume the cat stance; he doesn't dare move, knowing my ankles are close to his jugular. I could end the fight right now.

There is a moment of threat, neither of us knowing the other's next move. I balance on his shoulders and move into the crane position, my arms above my head, lifting my right knee to my chest. As I look out into bruised clouds and a limitless sky, my fear vanishes. My ninja training has taught me that I can create whatever I wish to see, whatever I wish to be. It is thoughts that hold you back, that create limits. If you want to make a change, you have to start with yourself. Thoughts are what fuel the change from normal to ninja.

Before I can leap off Hero's shoulders, his foot reaches up and smashes into my nose. The bones crunch and I fall backwards, rolling out to the edge of the platform.

'Had enough?' he calls from the centre of the circle.

I stand slowly and walk towards him. We face each other, bloodied and bruised.

'It doesn't have to be like this,' I say.

Hero shakes his head. 'The power of the scrolls belongs to the samurai.'

'They belong to the White Warrior,' I say.

'Show me the White Warrior!' he yells, opening his arms.

He flies at me with staccato strikes — knife hands, hammer fists, body punches, double upper blocks. I block them, catch his right hand among the flurry, lift it into a submission hold, applying pressure to his wrist and immobilising him. I wait for his face to contort with pain, then push-kick into his ribs with the ball of my right foot. I feel my birthmark growl and my toes hook like tiger claws. My powers are astonishing; my speed and accuracy improve each minute. At first, my abilities freaked me out, but now I understand.

'She's right here!' I say.

In the distance below, I see the glowing tombstone again, a mere pearl in the ocean of darkness. We are in a different realm here, but out there, somewhere, are the people I love. I am fighting for them.

I leap off my supporting leg into the air and smash into Hero's chest with a jumping side kick. He ploughs backwards and I follow up with a back fist to his cheek. His head whips to the side, but he regains his composure quickly and grabs my right foot and levers it up. I use the momentum to power a backflip and kick my left foot into his chin as I land. I kiss my ninja star and say, 'Come back to me,' then I flick the *shuriken* towards his eyes, the serrated blades spinning.

I assume a tiger stance, my right leg bent, my left leg straight, my hands in a water sign position, and watch Hero's eyes widen as the star closes in. He shuts his lids in anticipation, but the ninja star veers past his nose and grazes his brow, drawing a fine scratch across his left eyebrow. Then it swings around and comes back to me.

Hero's eyes slowly open. He touches them, feels the drip of blood on his forehead, then looks at me, confused. His eyes are less wild. He no longer looks like my enemy but a scared teenager.

I walk up to him and stand before him, not weak but strong and triumphant. He makes no attempt to move, staying seated beneath me.

The earth tower crumbles around us, lowering back down to the Cemetery of Warriors. Within seconds everything is back to normal. I walk over to the glowing tombstone and pick up the Tiger Scrolls. I smooth my hand over the book's leather binding and open its cover. Inside sit the five translucent scrolls, shimmering. I lift them to my nose and smell fire, wind, earth, water and nothingness.

The blue smoke of the circle thickens. I hear a footstep behind me ... I spin and duck out of the way of the *katana* sword.

As Hero charges again, I backflip to the edge of the circle. He takes a leaping step, then flies in a side kick towards me. I throw my ninja star at him, but I am too slow. I have just enough time to draw my tiny poisoned darts out of my belt and enough energy for a single breath to spit a dart towards him. The dart pierces his shoulder. He falls backwards.

'You are the White Warrior,' he says. 'But I am not the last samurai.'

Then he closes his eyes and disappears.

TWENTY-TWO

Hearing the words out loud sets all my instincts screaming. I turn to the ancient ninja's Tiger Scrolls; they are soaked in my blood. The sky is no longer burning red; it has returned to black velvet with the glow of the green moon. I lift one of the scrolls out of the book and it burns my finger. I ignore the pain to study it more closely. The scroll glows like a diamond against the curtain of night.

'The White Warrior will consume the power of the scrolls,' I say, remembering the legend.

I realise the scrolls are made of rice paper. I swallow hard, then quickly place the first scroll, Fire, on my tongue, relieving my burning finger. It dissolves in a burst of spiky heat, tasting like hot stone. I place the Wind Scroll on my tongue and it blasts down my throat, swift and sweet. The Earth Scroll tastes of grass; the Water Scroll turns to liquid and slides easily into my stomach. The Invisibility Scroll tastes of rice paper and

I have to chew to get it down. My body fills with savage energy as the five elements digest in my system. I feel their power in my heart.

I close my eyes. Every move of every martial art that ever existed fills my mind: the degrees of kicks, angles of blocks, sequences of movements lock in the private dojang of my heart. The powers of every ancient warrior dissolve into my spirit.

Suddenly, a scream rages from outside the circle. 'Roxyyyy!'

'Mum?'

I turn to see her sprinting towards me. Before I can react, I am clasped in her arms. Her hug torches the cemetery with light. Her orchid perfume washes away the putrid stench of death. The night creeps back into the circle. We step apart, but she keeps a firm grip on my hand.

'Mum, I beat the warriors. I took back my powers. I'm the White Warrior, Mum — the mark on my sole. Why didn't you tell me?' My voice is crisp beneath the canopy of night.

Mum glances at the empty book of Tiger Scrolls. Her eyes widen to black saucers. 'Where are they?' she gasps, realising what I have done.

A deafening chime from deep within me blasts the cemetery apart and forces Mum and me to the ground.

I roll onto my back as the sound roars out of my mouth and thunders over us in waves that crack the graves and sweep the remaining blue smoke from the circle.

'What's that?' I scream, commando-crawling over to her. The echoes are too strong for me to stand.

'The Tiger Scrolls singing!' she yells back.

As suddenly as the sound began, it stops. We rise slowly to our feet and dust off our ninja uniforms.

Mum looks at me with tears in her eyes.

'Once the scrolls are consumed, they sing to the sword of every samurai who has ever lived,' Mum says. The darkness moves into her eyes. 'Oh, Roxy, you have unleashed the Endless Fight.'

I swallow razor blades. We will never be safe now ...

Glossary

Axe kick — when a straightened leg descends onto an opponent like the blade of an axe.

Back kick — a kick backwards, like a donkey.

Dojang — sacred place of Taekwondo practice.

Dojo — secret place of ninja and samurai training.

Flying kick — any kick that involves air, usually accompanied with a running start then a huge jump.

Front kick — a kick forwards to the groin, stomach or face with the ball of your foot. Keep the toes out of it — they break easy.

Hook kick — a kick that strikes from the side using the heel of the foot. Executed similarly to a side kick, but aimed slightly off target and propelling backwards.

Kaki — fire tools.

Katana — a type of sword.

Ninja — known for wearing the best uniform in the business, ninjas were members of a feudal Japanese society of mercenary agents, highly trained in martial arts and stealth, for covert purposes ranging from espionage to sabotage and assassination. Also refers to anyone super cool.

Ninja claws — spikes worn between toes, fingers or teeth; used to climb, wound horses or slash enemies.

Ninjaing — gettin' ya ninja on.

Ninjaism — turning ninja.

Nunchucks — hand weapons used for frontal assault, consisting of two sticks joined by a chain.

Roundhouse kick — the hero of all martial arts kicks. The leg swings sideways in a circular motion to kick the enemy in the stomach with the instep of the foot or, if you are more of a street fighter, the shin. You can amp up your martial arts street cred by adding a 360-degree turn or even a 720-degree turn, and if you're really hardcore, a 1080 turn.

Sageo — the cord attached to a sword.

Samurai — the ninja's enemy. They are warriors who fight with swords. Super deadly. Not as cool. Love to wear red.

Shinobi shozoku — the traditional ninja all-black uniform.

Shuriken — a throwing blade or ninja stars.

Side kick — a sideways kick using the blade of your foot. You can show off by performing a double or triple side kick.

Tabi — two-toed sock shoes with a gap between the big toe and the rest of the toes; similar to webbed shoes.

Taekwondo — a Korean martial art and the national sport of South Korea. In Korean, *tae* means 'to strike with foot'; *kwon* 'to strike with fist'; and *do* 'method', or 'path'. Taekwondo is 'the way of the hand and the foot'. It combines combat techniques, self-defence, sport, exercise, board breaking, step-sparring, yelling, patterns, meditation and philosophy.

Torinoke — blown birds' eggs filled with gunpowder.

White Warrior — a ninja who can control the elements, flash invisible and fly.

Zukin — a ninja hood.

Acknowledgements

Thank you to the HarperCollins team of ninjas, including my inspiring publisher, Lisa Berryman; agent Clare Forster; and editors Nicola O'Shea and Kate Burnitt.

Lisa, thank you for believing in me, ninja and Gate Two kids everywhere.

To my brother, Lleyton, and beautiful sister, Bridget.

Thanks to Ed, what a nice Ed.

And to my parents, Martin and Jeanette Hall, who are the original White Warriors. Thank you for not freaking out when I told you I wanted to be a writer — full time. Mum and Dad, you are the ink in these words.

Roxy Ran also gets
her ninja on in ...